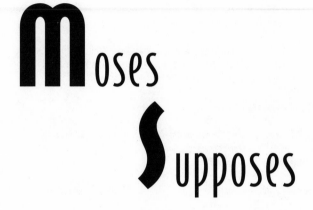

Moses Supposes

Ellen Currie

SIMON & SCHUSTER
New York London Toronto
Sydney Tokyo Singapore

SIMON & SCHUSTER
Rockefeller Center
1230 Avenue of the Americas
New York, New York 10020

Designed by Deirdre C. Amthor

Manufactured in the United States of America

10 9 8 7 6 5 4 3 2 1

Library of Congress Cataloging in Publication Data

Currie, Ellen.
Moses supposes / Ellen Currie.
p. cm.
I. Title.
PS3553.U667M67   1994
813' .54—dc20   93-47453
CIP

ISBN: 0-671-65673-2

The author is grateful to the John Simon Guggenheim Memorial Foundation and
the New Jersey State Council for the Arts.

"Tib's Eve" originally appeared in *The New Yorker* in 1958.

"O Lovely Appearance of Death" was first published by *The Dial* in 1959.

"Moses Supposes" was first published in the *New American Library of World
Literature* in 1958.

"Whatever You Say, Say Nothing" was first published by *New Directions* in 1977.

"On the Mountain Stands a Lady" was first published by *Accent* in 1956.

"Slim Young Woman in No Distress" was first published in *Canto* in 1978.

For the ones I love the best.

Comedy is the indirect praise of perfection.
—*Unknown*

Contents

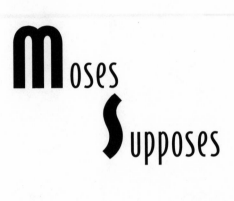

Yesterday's Lilies, Dollar a Stem. An Epsilon

Griffith finds a coil of rubber tubing in the cellar, handy to the gas water-heater. He takes it away and says nothing. The next night, fortified by the presence of the family dog, he finds another coil of tubing and he takes that one away, again without remark. The third night he and the dog find a hangman's noose, or what looks like one, fastened to a cellar beam. When Griffith finds the rope, he begins to shake with fear and pure exasperation.

Now he goes into the kitchen, where his tiny mother, Violet, called Shorty, though not by him, is on her knees scrubbing the floor. She whaps away as though the floor is filthy, but nothing in Violet's house is allowed to get even mildly, companionably dirty.

"Has Dad been worse lately?" Griffith asks.

Violet snorts and blows her loose, dyed, pony bangs off her nose. Asthmatic, she is nonetheless using a powerful solution of ammonia on the floor. Its fumes have her wheezing. The delicate skin of her unprotected arms and hands blazes. Griffith feels he is supposed to chide her for abusing herself, or anyway to take verbal note of these abuses so she can snub him. Instead he stands and stares at her. The dog, a pretty greyhound, reclines against his legs and stares at Violet, too, though with greater admiration.

Violet dyes only the front of her hair, the area she can see herself. She is proud of this habit and he is struck for the first time not by the quaintness of it, but by its wickedness, the contempt it reveals. The undyed white frowsy top of his mother's head is mooning him.

He is also irritated by the way she is clothed. She wears old finery for household chores, wringing, in her view, the last drop of use from it. But why? Her ruined dress is dangerously short; scintillating elfin green, it gleams with inappropriate playfulness. It is not a dress to be worn by an aging woman, his mother, whose aging husband, his father, plots suicide. Once, long ago, Griffith seems to remember Violet wearing this scrap of a dress—a gift of her then employer—to some function of point to him. On her feet at that time were peculiarly unsuitable shoes, also handed on to her by the rich, much younger, idiotic woman she worked for. Greatly complimented for the charm of her appearance on that day, Violet preened and pranced. Griffith thought she looked like a praying mantis.

"Get Princess out of the wet," Violet orders.

"The dog is fine," Griffith says, though he knows it upsets his parents to hear Princess, the only member of the family with whom everyone is on good terms, the only one granted unprovisional allegiance, spoken of as "the dog." And Princess, in fact, is dancing up to Violet to dab her with kisses, leaving clover marks on the wet smelly floor.

"Step back," Violet warns, menacing Griffith's shoe with her scrub brush.

"I asked you if Sammy's been worse," Griffith says, though he would like to ask her how he could have been born to such parents.

"Worse than what?" Violet says, with her customary bitterness. "Ask him does he want fish or chicken."

"Has he seemed more than usually depressed? I have a reason for asking."

"I'll give him what to be depressed about," Violet says. "Depressed, is it? Depressed, how are ye?"

"Nice lilies," Griffith says, to lighten her mood. Violet loves flowers and grows them, though she'd never cut her own flowers for the house. "I could do it," she says, when the possibility is mentioned, "but it would be wrong." These lilies, white and yellow ones, burgeon from a marmalade jar, though the house is full of porcelain containers. Chipped, cracked, missing members, these are gifts of the same ex-employer who gave her the deplorable dress. "They'd be worth a good penny," Violet says reverently of them, "if they was whole."

Griffith has given his mother vessels of various materials and his first wife, a fiber artist and potter, has given her many more, but none has stirred much enthusiasm. Still, "Nice lilies," Griffith says.

"Yesterday's lilies, dollar a stem," Violet says, grimly de-

———

fiant, as though he has accused her of some criminal undertaking, as though he has accused her of extravagance and guile. Or perhaps she is frightened—of age or poverty. Or perhaps she is darkly proud of buying down-market, low-end lilies, perhaps it shows her cleverness, her survival skills. God help him, he will never know.

"You don't have to buy yesterday's lilies," Griffith says. He gives her money regularly, and also irregularly, when he can't think of anything else to do. His fear is that she saves it, in full expectation of his failure, and will one day give it all back to him.

"I do, but," Violet says, which seems to end the audience. "Ask him fish or chicken."

•　　•　　•

In the silent, darkened living room, Griffith's little father sits alone. He moves his lips as though talking to himself, purses them as though whistling an inaudible song, but if he is speaking or mouthing a tune, Griffith has never been able to make out what it is he says or sings.

"Pop," Griffith says. "Dad."

"Whale it is," says Sammy. "Well named. The noise of you, blundering about."

Griffith, who in fairness and in fact has made no racket entering the room, is used to this, or as used to it as he is likely to get. Violet and Sammy are small people and Griffith is a large person, though not freakishly so. His parents have never been able to countenance the disparity in size, nor can they imagine, as they seem to need to, the machinery by which it came about. Violet is inclined to blame Griffith's size on some pills she was taking, knowing no better, as she says, at the time. During Violet's sacrificial pregnancy and Griffith's colossal birth, his parents called him The Whale. It may be their only shared joke and it is certainly too good to let go of. Griffith has several advanced degrees, he is a differential algebraist with an academic appointment at a nearby university; he has done some, not a lot, but some, original work. Still, when he was a boy, heroic in size, to hear them tell it, much worrying was done aloud. Could so large a child be "right"? When he began to show early signs of, if not brilliance, surely excellence in science and math, his parents, products of poor Belfast neighborhoods, ejected into the world at school-leaving age—fourteen, sixteen—pronounced his progress, cautiously, "not too bad."

Griffith sits down next to his father and crosses his legs. "I want to talk to you," he says. He is trying for a tone that is matey. His legs seem very long and his elevated foot very big.

"Get your big blutchers of boots from before my face, do," his father says. "You haven't wanted to talk to me since you got your education."

Griffith knows he has no gift for intimate exchange. He has had two wives and has two children, all of them average in stature, none of them brighter or duller than the general run, all unhappy with him in one way or another, all of them given to calling him Whale. He uncrosses his legs. "Are you feeling worse?" he asks his father.

"Worse than what?" Sammy says. It is the family mode.

"I mean, not any better?" Griffith says. He tries to hold on to the dog, but she deserts him for Sammy, who pulls her ears and loves her up. "I mean, how is your depression?" What kind of question is that, he thinks. How is

---

your depression? Worse? Better? About the same? Explain your answer.

"Depression, is it?" Sammy says. He turns on his son what seems to be a look of enmity. "I've no clean Y-fronts," he says despondently. "All me Y-fronts is soiled and Shorty knows it."

"Jockey shorts," Griffith says helplessly. All his life he's been compelled to set his parents straight on American usage. All it ever gets him is trouble.

He is horrified to see his father's eyes fill with tears.

"Y-fronts, Y-fronts, I know what you mean," Griffith says. "I'm sure she's planning to do a big wash before she sees her bed tonight." Doing a big wash before she sees her bed is one of Violet's specialties. "Are you taking your pills?"

"Pills," Sammy says. Again, it is the family style, which combines no information with loathing.

"I was prescribed antidepressant pills after Diane, actually," Griffith says. "After Dawn, too, I believe. I didn't find them all that useful." This does not seem to be a profitable line of discourse. "But authorities agree that they can be. In certain cases." He had, after Dawn, and then again after Diane, put his faith in chemistry and chemistry had failed him.

"That first wee girl was a nice wee girl, but no, Whale, you couldn't stick her," Sammy says. He liked Dawn, the fiber artist, because she brought him elegant photographs of beautiful things: hinges, gates, simple articles of everyday utility exquisitely wrought in iron. Sammy is a farrier, a shoer of horses, a blacksmith. Dawn wanted him to express himself splendidly in manipulated iron, a material about which she entertained mystical feelings. Sammy kept

———

all the photographs and flirted heavily and obscurely with Dawn but so far as Griffith knows has never made of iron other than a horseshoe. "Sure," he would say to Dawn, of some thrilling screen or stile, "she"—meaning Shorty— "would only throw it in a corner."

"Dawn left me," Griffith says, "because, she claimed, I didn't anticipate her needs." This is as close as he has ever come to a confidence with his father.

"Och, aye," says Sammy, as though that would have been his own assessment.

"I find her statement unintelligible," Griffith says.

"Och, aye," says Sammy, as before.

"Diane left me," Griffith says, "because, this is only the proximate cause, but it gives you the tenor of the relation- ship, because I let it slip that I simply do not believe in the doctrine, if I may so phrase it, of the unconscious. You re- member, no doubt, that Diane is a family therapist."

"Aye," Sammy says. Diane had presented Violet and Sammy with chapter and verse on the family dynamic. Griffith was never able to tell if it made any dent. "Nice wee girl," Sammy says. "Fat ass on her like the hind end of a bus, but."

"That's so," Griffith says. "Could I have the dog for a while? You've had her for your turn."

Sammy strokes Princess and looks into the distance. His head tilts in a way Griffith hates, the angle makes Sammy look sly and cringing. Probably he is obliged to cock his head that way because of an old injury. Sammy has been kicked and rolled on, stepped on, bitten, by legendary horses and by losers. The imprint of a horse's hoof is stamped upon his brow. The hoof missed smashing the bony orbit around his eye by the tiniest measure, as Sammy is fond of demonstrating, whacking himself with his fist to do so. "That close," Sammy says, when he does this, "by less than one sixty-fourth of an inch. By how much would you reckon that, Whale, you being a mathematical professor?" he said once, and Griffith, irritated, because Sammy mocks his passion and points to Griffith's poor arithmetic when possible, answered, "Epsilon. An arbitrarily small positive number greater than zero." Ever after, Sammy has boasted of missing blindness by "an epsilon."

"I was a man, once," Sammy says. He says this in an insufferable overrehearsed way, but Griffith knows what he means and that his pain is real enough.

"Any man can lose his job," Griffith says. "I could lose my own." Indeed, he could lose his job, and his career if it comes to the point, having been charged by separate, equally plausible, equally deluded students of sexual harassment and racial bias. His ex-wives find these accusations preposterous and, evidently, hilarious. None of his friends is appropriately outraged, although his friends know what could lie in store for him and the tedious, exhausting route to it. His parents do not know of the charges. He is guiltless but ashamed before them. The prospect of explaining political correctness, academic dilemmas, anything at all, to Violet and Sammy daunts him. Actually, he would rather put his head in an oven.

"I was a man once," Sammy says again, and this time it doesn't go down so well.

"Oh, for Christ's sake," Griffith says, "you didn't expect to go into the sunset shoeing racehorses and polo ponies for rich people, did you? There aren't that many rich people, or that many racehorses. The rich have short attention spans."

———

"I was thirty-four years with him. That isn't a drop in the bucket. The man knew horses."

"Allow me," Griffith says. "You loved him like a son." He has heard this all his life. Personally, Griffith is afraid of horses and sees very little point to them. "If the man knew horses, how did the man lose all his goddamn money on them?"

"Indeed, I never loved him like a son," Sammy says. "He was a drunken whoremaster. But they was lovely stables."

"Well, they're part of a lovely community college now," Griffith says. "Covered already with spray-paint graffiti. Allegations of racial and gender bias. Unfounded, probably."

"Herself was not generous to your mother," Sammy says. Herself was the latest horsey wife, and this one hadn't hit it off well with Violet. But, as usual, Violet had fetched and carried, cleaned and cooked, pinned up hems and nannied, filling in when cannier staff fled the territory. All the while Judy to Sammy's Punch. Forelock pulling, tireless, cutely contentious, nothing inconvenient, mind. Irish. Characters. Pets. For one three-year period, Violet and Sammy did not speak to each other at all. They left notes on the mantelpiece, their hollow tree. They addressed remarks to the dog, not this dog, a boxer, greatly mourned. "Ask your mistress should I bring home fish or chicken." "Tell your master I don't give a damn." Their employers never noticed their silence, because they were hectic and merry in company, because they concealed this backstairs misery.

When the squire, as Sammy used to call him, sold up, he gave Sammy a sum of money, not a large sum considering the thirty-four years, and a great deal of advice. Griffith gave Sammy advice of his own. Sammy listened to neither of them. Instead he blew the money on an elaborately fit-

———

ted van. The van has "Wee Sammy, Farrier" painted on its side and a tiny jigging figure dressed in singlet and kilt. What this figure has to do with Irish Sammy's inner life, Griffith would prefer not to know. The van has not been out of the driveway. When Griffith persuaded Sammy to take him for a spin, the battery proved dead. The look on the triple A guy's face was something to behold. Violet's farewell gifts gave her more satisfaction. They were a large paste brooch with a defective clasp and a great big shiny handbag in a curious, even by Violet's standards, color.

Violet often shows the brooch, saying, "Wouldn't I look grand wearing that? Pinned to me bosom and me on my knees scrubbing floors."

Griffith hates to hear her talk this way, because he has heard it before, when he's given Violet bits of quite nice jewelry. Why, he wonders, does she see herself as a woman who has no life but scrubbing floors and hates this destiny? The handbag hurts Violet's feelings, and his own, but not in the same way. "The poor wee scut, she had no breeding," Violet says of its donor, "and if I'm not mistaken, a touch of the schizofrenzy."

"Your mother, of course, is not right in the mind," Sammy says. This is a beloved family theme, each of his parents interpreting any given action of the other's as personal malice plus madness of a more general kind.

Sammy disappears for many unexplained hours, never speaks directly to Violet, poisons with salt the food she is cooking when she turns aside, raises and lowers flames beneath pots, turns off the oven when dinner is half-baked in it, and defends himself when challenged for these actions on the grounds that he is something called the master of the home and can, therefore, presumably reflecting his experience of masters, do as he likes, however lunatic his whim.

Griffith also remembers, forcibly, looking at Sammy, pathetic as you like, but bullet-headed, powerful in his upper body, days and nights when Sammy used his fists and feet on Violet, days when he ripped the phone from the wall and flung it through an unopened window because Violet made so bold as to try to notify the police that she was streaming with blood and in danger of her life. Griffith remembers the day, it is a day upon which he heard his father described as "darling," when he saw his father thrust his mother down a flight of cellar stairs. In this house. He remembers that she was coated, afterward, with sticky stuff from tape and red Mercurochrome, a useless substance. He, a little boy, was summoned to her tubside to try to scrub the stains from her milky skin. She covered her nakedness with folded arms and washcloths. He remembers her slippery body, and their mutual shame and the smell of hot water and Ivory soap. He wanted then to kill his father and, in a quite uncharacteristic burst of courage, told him so. Mostly, though, a prissy little boy, he impressed his father with the likelihood of punishment and disgrace, should Griffith, then about twelve, spread it around that Sammy was a wife-beater. Can it really be that no one knew?

"You are not to harm yourself," he says sternly to Sammy.

"I'll do as I like," says Sammy automatically.

"Do as you like, then," Griffith says, impressed with his own toughness, "but not in my mother's house. It's obscene. You are not to subject her to that, do you understand? I don't give a damn how depressed you are."

———

"Man, dear," Sammy says, "I haven't a clue what you're talking about."

"Fish or chicken?" Griffith says.

"You were very fond of us when you were a wee boy."

"I'm still very fond of you, goddamn it. Fish? Chicken?"

"I'm not fussy about fish," Sammy says. "Nor chicken either should it come to that."

"No more am I," Griffith says. "Still, fish or chicken?"

He makes whimpering, seductive noises back in his throat and when that doesn't work, he leaps to his feet and shouts, "Walkies? Walkies?" at Princess until she removes her nose from Sammy's armpit and follows Griffith from the room.

●　　●　　●

Violet prepares an excellent meal and slams it on the table to them as though she were hurling it against the wall. When he has eaten it, Griffith goes to call on the medievalist he is courting. Her adolescent children are rude to him and she excuses this by suggesting that they are, in fact, rude to everyone. He and the medievalist drink too much, quarrel, fall into bed, where nothing goes properly. The medievalist, a pinched little beauty in homespun and lariats of amber beads, points out that he does not love her. He confirms this and adds that he finds himself smothered in people clamoring to be loved and declining to be lovable. He includes himself in this company. She shouts at him for a very long time, drawing examples from her field of special interest that he is not able to follow. Shortly after daylight, her children throw him out.

When he gets back to his parents' house, he finds it

empty. Violet is gone. Sammy is gone. Princess is gone. The van is gone, too, which seems to offer a ray of hope, though a feeble one. Have they all made off together to begin life anew? Elsewhere? Not too bloody likely.

He looks for them, but only in the house. He eats things from Violet's refrigerator and piles dirty dishes in Violet's sink. He drinks up Sammy's rotgut and the cordials he has brought his mother through the years. In the afternoon, drunk, sick, tearful, and chattering with fear, he approaches the telephone to call someone. Who? As he ponders this—he has been pondering it of course for many hours—the telephone rings and on it is the voice of Spaldeen. Ned something, actually, but when they were in high school, Ned was called Spaldeen. He admired girls with little, round, hard breasts. Whale admired girls with big, soft, floppy ones. Spaldeen tells Whale that Violet has been found in a park beneath a tree. Her clavicle is cracked and something's funny with her knee, but other than that, says Ned/Spaldeen, she's perfectly okay. Already won their hearts at the hospital, full of beans, a sketch, a character. Princess was tied to another tree, barking. A report of unattended dog, barking, brought the cops. So Princess may have saved her life, or anyway, her clavicle, her knee.

"Jesus," Griffith says.

"I'm sorry, Whale, there's more. Your old man's been arrested."

"Good."

"I did what I could, it's nothing much, but you know Wee Sammy. Feisty. You shouldn't let him mess with the shop up in the woods, you know, fire."

This is mysterious to Griffith. What shop? What woods? What fire? And then he remembers that long ago Sammy

———

21

had a smithy shack back in the woods. Woods now largely given over to a shopping mall. Surely, that shop has been derelict for years. Ned/Spaldeen is rattling on about fond memories of the shop in the woods, a teenage drunk that Sammy let him sleep off up there. Griffith remembers the shop in the woods as a scary place, all sweat and stink and fire.

"I hate that man, I'd like to kill his ass," Griffith says.

"Naw, Whale, I didn't hear that. You should've been there, he had made this thing, a lamp I think it is, it might be a lamp, I could be wrong, out of horseshoes. Jesus, Whale, happy as a frog and drunk as a duck. He's a character, he's a stitch. He hit my deputy, bonged his earlobe, mashed his nose. Assault."

"Lock him up, Spaldeen, you'll be doing him a favor. He'll dine out on it."

Griffith believes he is listening closely as Ned tells him how to reclaim his loved ones. All he takes in, though, is how and where to get the dog. He feels peculiarly careless and happy. He has heard that people who have decided to end their lives feel this way, free and fated.

He takes the hangman's rope from its hiding place in his closet and drives to the pound to pick up Princess, who greets him with her high, habitual glee.

Together, they drive to the park where his mother was found. It is no distance from the house, a few minutes' walk, he could easily have found her himself. He and the dog patrol the paths. There is no likely tree, no crime scene tape, no piteous length of clothesline, no bed of rumpled leaves. There is an abandoned wire shopping cart with a baby seat in it and a sign on the seat that says "Reserved for Tomorrow's Customers." He knows very well that Violet made no

---

serious attempt to kill herself. She would never have done such a thing in front of the dog. The dog, however, is hoarse. He thinks of Violet lying there—where?—somewhere here, hurting in her kneecap and her collarbone, listening to Princess bark for hours. He picks a tree, just any tree, and loops the hangman's rope over a branch, climbing on the shopping cart to do so. It is a shoddy affair, the hangman's rope, makeshift as these things go. He puts his head through the noose and kicks the shopping cart away.

His weight snaps the limb as he had thought it would and dumps him on his backside on the ground. Princess leaps into his arms and they roll there in the dirt, laughing.

———

Moses
Supposes

The first thing Patrick heard that morning, in his mother-in-law's damp, cold, closed-up beach house, was the crash and stammer of the air-locked shower on the floor beneath his room. He lay catty-corner on an iron bed, more or less under a sandy and dilapidated quilt. He was sunburned and gloomy and twenty years old. There were no sheets on the bed and neither it nor the quilt was adequate to his length. He was freezing.

The person taking the shower was Patrick's wife, Mona. He had met her the summer before last in this same seaside village, where he'd worked as a waiter at the Balmy Days Hotel. Since he had no money and no daring, considered himself to be low on charm, and came equipped with a record of debacle in dealings with children, small animals, and girls, he'd thought for a while that being in love with Mona was the worst thing that ever hit him. They made a ludicrous couple. She was a little, noisy, pretty girl; a sort of blue jay, heretical, put together by a reckless hand. He was peripheral—horribly tall, ferocious, and shy. He knew that he didn't have a chance. But then one winter night, in the Lion's Den back at Columbia, she'd said rather tragically over a grilled cheese sandwich that she thought they'd better get married; so they had. Eight months later she surreptitiously departed from their "studio" apartment on 115th Street, taking with her the dress she was married in and nearly all the joy he had ever known.

That had been on Monday. Her mother called Patrick Monday night, to tell him that Mona was perfectly fine, but incommunicado. By Tuesday he was breathing fast and had managed to loosen all his lower front teeth. On Wednesday his mother-in-law, who had an aptitude for intrigue, threw out a tip that enabled him to track Mona. But here it was Thursday, and he had yet to set eyes on her.

He'd walked up from the station on Wednesday afternoon with his hands in his pockets and his heart in his mouth. He found the door unlocked and the house deserted. It was a peculiar house, a partly dismantled shrine to a former owner, a man named Dizzy Bailey, who seemed to have been a comedian of the baggy-pants school. Now and then Mona's mother carted away some of the theatrical memorabilia and stowed it in a closet underneath the stairs, but for the most part she contended herself with supplementing the decor—she ran to bathrooms papered with *Punch* covers, pieces of batik tacked up on walls, and lamps converted from champagne jeroboams. The living room was two stories high and in addition to it the first floor contained a kitchen, a bedroom, and a bath. Patrick went into that bedroom. A few of Mona's things were there. On the second floor, five more bedrooms opened off a mezzanine. Distributed among them, in a fairly carefree fashion, were seventeen uncomfortable beds, several of them double-deckers. Dizzy Bailey had liked to have people around him, and so did Mona's mother.

Patrick had sat around for a while—stranded in the godforsaken whimsicality of the living room, having a crisis of nerves and sweating forlornly in the Indian summer heat. Then he hung the somber suit his father had bought him for a trousseau proprietorially in Mona's closet. He'd discovered a derelict pair of bathing trunks on the porch, and he put them on. The weather was freakish—too warm for fall, but never quite as warm as you thought it was, and far too cold for bathing trunks.

Stippled with gooseflesh and rejoicing in his own discomfort, Patrick toured the beachfront, searching for Mona. He didn't find her. In fact, he didn't see anyone at all, and he was in no mood for looking at oceans. The houses he could see were shuttered and desolate. There was no one fishing in the surf. There was no girl sitting out on the end of the jetty, where he'd first seen Mona, alone and cross-legged, her face toward Spain.

He plowed along through the soft sand of the dunes, exploring his character. He had it in for himself and he didn't see why Mona shouldn't, too. He drafted quite a bill of particulars: He decided it was high time he figured out whether he was going to be Saint Francis or a man of steel; he decided that although he was six feet four inches tall, he was skinny as a rail and astigmatic and probably not even, if you could believe what people told you, very virile. He was a prig and a grind; he was sulky; he was sentimental. All the A's and 99s and Excellents and Splendids he'd ever aspired to, ever won, were tattooed on his chest. He belonged in skirts, a sprig of lilac pinned to his collar, tears in his eyes. He saw right through himself, and he didn't see why Mona shouldn't.

By the time he'd gotten it all worked out, he was a million miles from nowhere. When he got back to the house, Mona's door was on the hook and his clothes were on the floor outside it. If he was any kind of a man, he said to himself as he stamped upstairs, he'd break down that door and swarm all over her. But it simply wasn't in him. He lay down on the first bed he came to. The last thing that assailed him before he fell almost instantly asleep was the terrible knowledge that his whole life, up to and including that day, had been a washout.

.   .   .

He had no real hopes for this chilly Thursday morning, either, but the disadvantages of his situation, plus the fact that he was hungry, changed yesterday's anguish to a kind of noble pessimism. Somewhat stiffened by it, he got up.

When he went downstairs and into the kitchen, Mona was scouring the sink. She was wearing an outsize track sweater and a pair of faded jeans. It was Patrick's track sweater. This circumstance so cheered him that he felt he'd been dropped, upright, several feet through space.

"Hello," he said politely.

"Hello, morose," Mona said without turning. She sluiced

water around the sink, squinted at it, and went to work
with the scouring powder again. All of this rub-a-dub-dub
looked awfully out of character to him.

He hooked his bare foot around the leg of an old bridge
chair painted turquoise and dragged it out from the table. It
made a satisfactory noise on the gritty floor. Mona didn't
look up. Patrick sat down, feeling conspicuous and unsightly,
but attracting remarkably little attention. He sneezed.

Mona looked at him then. "Is that sunburn?" she asked,
in a tone that played scorn against repulsion.

"No," Patrick said, which was a lie. He was susceptible
to scrofulous, peeling sunburns, of the type that never
turned to tan. This condition called up in him a dispropor-
tionate sense of shame. He sneezed again.

"Have you got a cold, too?" Mona wanted to know. She
was taking on a certain air of menace.

"Yes, I have a cold, too," Patrick said. "It's all part of my
death wish."

Mona put the can of scouring powder down on the table
beside him. It was called Bon Ami. He was moved almost
to tears.

"I'm sort of hungry," he said pitifully.

"You can't feel too bad if you're hungry."

"Since when did you know how I feel? You never know
how I feel."

"You never know how I feel, either," Mona said. "You
only know how *you* feel; you never know how *I* feel."

"That's true," Patrick said. The conversation appeared
to him to be going into a skid. He propped his elbows on
the table and his head on his hands. He was cold, feverish,
sore, miserable. He cared more about this girl than any-

thing he could think of, and he couldn't even talk to her.
She jogged his elbows off the table and swabbed it with a
damp cloth. He sat with his clasped hands caught between
his bare and hairy knees and inventoried, bleakly, the shelf
above the kitchen table. He counted three different brands
of oregano, all of the possible permutations of garlic, a
corkscrew, a bottle of bitters, some smelling salts, and a jar
of face cream, which numbered among its ingredients not
only estrogenic hormones but royal jelly, right, so to speak,
from the mouth of the queen bee. All those things reminded him of his mother-in-law. His mother-in-law had
married four times. He reflected that Mona had a dreadful
heredity. And her environment had been nothing to brag
about.

"You don't need hormones, kiddy," Patrick said mourn-
fully.

"What's that supposed to mean?" Mona said. She was
busy with a broom now. She'd been holding it like a hockey
stick, but she switched her grip, the better, possibly, to
swat him with it.

"You swing that thing at me and I'll smack you so hard,
you'll fly up to the ceiling," he warned her.

"If you think I came out here with somebody else, you're
out of your mind," Mona said. "Try that on for size."

It was a thought that hadn't crossed his mind, but it did
so now, with painful heat. "I know you from the old country," he shouted. "Try that on for size!"

"I just want to tell you one thing," Mona said, poking
her head at him and leaning tensely on her broom. "I came
out here to get my mind off my mind, that's the only reason. And I was doing all right until you showed up. Now

———

put your *clothes* on and don't keep *shivering*."

"Not me," Patrick said. His clothes were still in a heap before her bedroom door; he'd seen them.

"If I make some scrambled eggs, will you put your clothes on?" Mona said blackly.

"No," Patrick said, after thinking it over.

"I suppose you came out here for a serious talk. Well, I can't have a serious talk with anybody that looks the way you do."

The wall behind Patrick had been covered, in a wayward decorative impulse, with straw hats hung on nails. Hats of all shapes and sizes hung there, in various colors and stages of decrepitude—hats that might have struck the taste of coolie laborers, Calvin Coolidge, members of calypso bands, middle-aged ladies on Caribbean cruises. Patrick selected a thing with a floppy fringed brim and a pink felt octopus wearing sunglasses fixed to its crown. Mona's mother had brought it home from Nassau. She thought it was a riot. Patrick stood up, bowed, clapped the hat on his head, brushed off his trunks, and generally put himself in order, all with a tight smile for his wife.

"Very funny," Mona said.

He suspected that she did think he was funny. He didn't think he was funny at all. He stalked into the living room and lay down on his back on the rattan couch. He pulled one of the loose cushions from the back of the couch and folded his arms across it. The cushion was lumpy and smelled of damp. He hugged it against the chill in the room, determined not to think about anything. He would not hold two opposing points of view at once; he would not examine both sides of any question; he would be stoic, ruthless, and hard.

———

Autographed photographs, programs, caricatures, cartoons, almost obliterated the board walls of the living room. They dated from Dizzy Bailey's time. Patrick studied them, prostrate. He was full of tender feelings as a rule, and chance mementos of other people's lives inflamed in him a counterfeit nostalgia—they seemed to offer hints of something panoramic, something poignant, meaningful, and large. Today, for no very clear reason, all that salvage, growing yearly more distant and irrelevant in its frames, disgusted him. He loathed it. Patrick looked up at the more-than-life-sized portrait of Dizzy Bailey that hung, suspended on lengths of cable, from the peak of the roof. It showed him, grinning, mugging, very ocher in complexion, behind bars. He was wearing a broadly striped convict's suit and a little round pillbox hat and a ball and chain on his ankle. Outside of the cell, taking stock of him, sat a tiny marcelled pompon of a dog. According to the written testimony of all these people in these glossy photographs, all these people who had licked their lips and smiled, Dizzy Bailey was a great little guy. For the first time, Patrick was prepared to doubt it. Dizzy Bailey looked pretty sinister, if you really looked at him. He looked sly. That dog, bellied down in a pose Patrick had mistaken for fidelity and trust, had Dizzy Bailey's number, that dog was wasting for a chance to sink its teeth in Dizzy Bailey. On the other hand, it knew, ball and chain or no, that Dizzy Bailey still had one free foot. Dizzy Bailey had been kicking that dog around for many a moon. Maybe. On the third hand, maybe not. If you looked at things one way, they were one thing. If you looked at them another way, they turned into something else. The force of this encounter with truth made Patrick's face hot, and he pulled his hat brim down

———

over his eyes, groaning. He listened to Mona banging things in the kitchen. Misery sat on his chest.

Then it began to rain, with a spatter like a handful of pebbles flung against the house. He reached out and plucked the string of an old standard lamp that stood behind the couch. The room was suddenly cozy, even warmer, lighted in the rain. In his present temper he was inclined to regret this. It happened that Mona thought that the use of electricity during rainstorms invited catastrophe, though, and he hoped to lure her into the living room to turn the lamp off. He latched his fingers across his eyes and watched the doorway to the kitchen through them. Before very long, Mona appeared there.

"Are you going to put on your clothes like a human being, or not?" she said aloofly.

"Not," Patrick said. She didn't look grieved, especially. "I'm not a human being, kiddy," Patrick said. "I'm just an old bone that's been thrown out of the cage."

"I don't mind it so much when you're just maladjusted," Mona said. "But when you're melancholy, that I resent." She wandered over to the lamp and made a fleeting pass at it, before she caught herself and put her hands behind her for a stroll around the room. "Raining," she announced, lighting on a window seat.

"You're uncannily correct," Patrick said. "Uncannily."

"It's cold in here," Mona said.

"Check," Patrick said.

Mona went over to his clothes, piled helter-skelter on the floor, and swung her foot in an arc across them. "I see you wore your blue shirt."

"So?" Patrick said.

"I happen to know you think you look pretty cute in your blue shirt."

"You don't know half what you think you know," Patrick said.

"I don't know anything, to hear you tell it," Mona said without rancor. "I don't know anything. I don't feel anything. Except the wrong things, of course." She stirred his clothes gingerly with the toe of her sneaker.

"Not at all," Patrick said, speaking up at the roof, "not at *all*. I know you're a fine type. Sensitive. I know you won that poetry prize at the Greek Games last year. I read that 'Lyric to Athena,' boy. I'm familiar with that picture of a clown you painted in your senior year at Music and Art."

"What's the matter with my clown?" Mona asked dangerously.

"Nothing's the matter with him. He's smashing. He's posh. I'm crazy about him myself. I just hate pictures of clowns, that's all. They're what everybody paints when they get their first insight."

"Thanks a big bunch," Mona said. She was considering his clothes, bent with her legs apart in a stance she might as well have employed to inspect a dead bat on a back road somewhere.

"I thought you were a truth seeker," Patrick said. "Or I wouldn't have brought it up."

She picked up his shirt by one cuff, swept it along the floor, and tossed it at him. It missed the couch and fell on the floor beside him with a light clatter of buttons against boards. He paid it no attention. She tossed his trousers at him, too, and they sailed completely over the couch, raining change, and landed on the other side. She dusted her hands and went back into the kitchen. He heard her thumping around out there. After a while she brought in a tumbler of orange juice and put it down on a battered table covered with snapshots of Dizzy Bailey, under glass. The orange juice was just out of reach. He left it there. She brought in a tray with a plate of scrambled eggs and some silver on it and put it beyond the orange juice.

"Just sit up and eat like a human being, will you," she said. "I don't want egg all over everywhere."

"I believe I can be trusted to eat a few scrambled eggs," Patrick said grandly, "without littering the whole country-side."

She went back into the kitchen and stayed there. He held his straw hat on his head with one hand and his cushion on his chest with the other and, with difficulty, raised the upper half of his body to shout: "Come in here!" Nothing happened. He sat up and swallowed two enormous fork-fuls of scrambled eggs, rearranging the rest to conceal the dent he'd made in them. Then he went into the kitchen, wearing his hat and carrying his cushion.

Mona was standing by the stove, holding a piece of toast between her teeth and taking off her jeans. She'd already taken off her sweater. She was wearing a lavender bathing suit, not her own. He could see on her shoulders the pale familiar streaks where last year's straps had crossed and these straps didn't. She folded the jeans and put them, with the sweater, on a chair. Then she took a big red dunce cap off the wall and put it on her head. Her hair was straight and fair and, he thought, pastoral. It stuck out from under the pointed hat in wisps, though, and she resembled an eighteen-year-old, inexperienced witch. She took a bite out of her toast and stood looking at him, not very friendly.

———

40

"Where's *my* toast?" Patrick said.

"I'm not using any toaster in this storm," Mona said. "I'm not electrocuting myself just to stuff you full of toast. This is yesterday's toast."

He knew her habit of saving scraps and dabs of this and that and consuming them, dutifully, days later. It made him uncomfortable, but it made him feel at home. His mother did it, too. He thought it was something basic in the female character. Something a little bit admirable and a little bit corrupt. Mona looked pathetic standing there, chewing on her old abandoned toast. Her summer tan was going fast and the cold brought a chalky bloom to her skin. She was also slightly bowlegged.

"I forgot my eggs," he said. He went into the living room, dropped his cushion on the couch, picked up his eggs and his orange juice, and stood in the doorway to bolt his breakfast while he watched her. He thought she looked unhappy and cold.

"Let's light the oven," he said.

"What for?"

"For the sport of the thing," he said. "Maybe we'll make a few loaves of toast. A lifetime supply of secondhand toast, wouldn't you like that?"

"Sure I would," Mona said. "Wouldn't anybody?"

"Anybody with his wits about him," Patrick said. He put down his empty plate and knelt in front of the stove. There was no pilot light for the oven, he had to ignite the gas with a match. He did this with considerable trepidation, half expecting to ignite the octopus on his hat and turn himself into a human torch. The gas caught with a pop, though, and no damage. He straightened up, leaving the oven door open. Mona was huddled on one of the turquoise bridge

———

chairs. She had her heels on the seat and her chin rested on her right knee. There was a big yellow bruise on her left shin and the area around her eyes was smudged with violet. She looked starved and fugitive in the darkening kitchen, like an underprivileged raccoon. Patrick wanted to turn on the overhead light, but in another way he didn't. He didn't want to affront her in any way, suddenly. He'd have gone, for the moment, way out of his way not to cause her any pain. It was raining very hard.

"Why don't you move your chair out into the middle of the room, baby," he said tenderly. "It'd be warmer."

"Don't call me that," Mona said.

"Listen, Mona," he began fretfully.

"Screw you," Mona said.

"What'd *I* do?" Patrick shouted. "What'd I *do?* I come home from a three-hour lab and you're gone. I find a note on the lamp shade. 'There's a lamb chop in the refrigerator'—I need a lamb chop like I need a third leg. How would you like it?"

"I guess I wouldn't like it," Mona said.

"I wouldn't do it to you," Patrick said.

"Well, I would do it to you and I did do it to you, so shut up."

"Everything was cotton candy and all of a sudden I'm no place. That's a fine way to treat me!"

"I'm sorry if I hurt your feelings," Mona said courteously. "I didn't mean it that way."

"Feelings, *feelings,*" Patrick bellowed. "Aren't you happy, or what?"

"The next son of a bitch that asks me am I happy, I'm going to spit in his eye," Mona said.

"I'd like to know where you got all this language,"

Patrick said, infuriated, "that's what I'd like to know."

"I'm a married woman and I can use any language I feel like," Mona told him. "I can use Esperanto if I feel like it. I can say any words I feel like." She gave him samples of words she felt like saying at the moment.

"Your mother should get a load of that," Patrick said.

"My mother," Mona said. She put her hands in the hair that straggled from under her hat and gave it a pull.

"Your mother's all right," Patrick said. "I don't like you when you act that way. Your mother's a great old girl."

"She walks, she talks, she crawls on her belly like a reptile," Mona said. "She's a great old girl."

"She figured out where you were, anyway."

"She figured out where I was because I told her. That's how smart she is. I told her not to tell you, of course. But she has no conception of honor whatsoever. What else did she tell you?"

"Plenty," Patrick said grimly, lying.

"Like what, for instance?" Mona asked, looking at him.

"Are you alone out here?" he said, feeling sick.

"In my estimation that's an extremely vile thing for you to say to me," Mona said haughtily. "And my mother never said anything like that to you, either. And you don't even believe it, which makes it worse."

"I don't know what all she said to me," Patrick said. "She said not to worry. That was pretty funny. She said men were different from women, which wasn't exactly news. She kept kissing me and crying and getting philosophical. I think she's reading Ouspensky again, she's all muddled up. I mean, more than always."

"Oh, the poor thing," Mona said.

"What about me? I'm the poor thing in this scenario."

———

43

"You're just so pure, you could die of it, Tiger."

"Why are you so mad at me?"

"Don't be wistful, you crumb," Mona said. "That's not significant." She picked up a waxed paper carton that had held orange juice, drained the last quarter inch into a glass, and shied the carton at a brown paper bag full of trash. The whole business toppled, dumping eggshells on the floor. "My garbage runneth over," she said sadly.

"*Our* garbage," Patrick said. He went over and cleaned up the mess.

"Pardon me," Mona said. "I forgot."

"I love you," Patrick said dismally, on his knees among the eggshells.

"I know it," Mona said, drinking her orange juice.

"Well then, don't you? I mean, love me?"

Mona shrugged. "That's not terribly significant, as I see it."

"If you run across anything that's significant," Patrick said, "I hope to Christ you'll let me know." The kitchen was getting very dark, despite the glow drifting in from the other room. He found two candle stubs set in clamshells on the drainboard. He lighted them and brought them over to the table. They made for a queer, rather ritual atmosphere. He sat down opposite Mona, scowling at her lack of appreciation of his efforts at homemaking. "Listen, Mona," he said, clearing his throat, "just tell me one thing. Don't get mad, now, just tell me one thing. Where were you yesterday when I was looking for you?"

"It's none of your business where I was. You have a dirty mind. I climbed a tree, if it's any of your business."

"A tree."

"You know what a tree is, Tiger. With leaves on. Not

that this was much of a tree, but it was all I could find on short notice. I just felt like sitting in a tree. Like I'd led a wasted life on account of not having sat in enough trees, or like I might not get another chance. Or I don't know, something wiggy. I was looking at bark. I hope you realize you're embarrassing me."

"Bark."

"You're acquainted with bark?"

"Bark," Patrick said, as though a great many things had straightened out for him. "I used to eat it." He put his hand across his eyes and squeezed them.

"Verree funnee," Mona said.

"I did," Patrick said guiltily. "We had a sweet cherry tree in the yard and I ate off all the bark as high as I could reach and then I piled stones around the trunk and ate more. It died, the tree."

"Are you riddled with remorse, by any chance?"

Patrick looked at her with real dislike. "I killed that tree. If that tree had been a man, they'd have hung me."

"I think that's pretty cute," Mona said in a nasty way.

"It doesn't exactly haunt me night and day."

"I think it's pretty cute the way your eyelids puff up when you look at those pictures of baskets of kittens."

"Carry on," Patrick said.

"I like the way you get religious when you see those old raggedy women raiding trash cans on Broadway. I like the way it makes you think of your mother and my mother and me. And all the time you know darn well your mother's playing mah-jongg in the Bronx and I'm eating sugar doughnuts in the snack bar at Barnard. And my mother, beloved wife of Tom, Dick, Harry, and Max, is over on the couch on Park Avenue, giving her analyst an earful."

"You have a deep understanding of my character," Patrick said unpleasantly. "You have some terrific insights at times."

"That's right."

"Okay," Patrick said. "If you want to be that way, *be* that way."

"If I gave you half a chance, you'd be one of those people who's always hauling other people around to look at sunsets and expecting them to vibrate when you vibrate. You're a truth and beauty monger, and I hate them all."

"Well, I'm very sorry," Patrick said formally, making wet, intersecting circles with the bottom of her glass, "but that's the way I am."

"I know how you are. I don't have to *like* it. I like the kind of people that keep a tommy gun in their violin case. That's the kind of people I like."

"Well, you married me," Patrick said bravely, "so you better get used to me."

"I'm no good at this married business; I'm very sorry, but I don't know the first thing about it. It was all a big mistake. One time after we got married I brought home some strawberries, regular strawberries in a box. And after I got them home, I didn't know *what* I was supposed to do with them. Do you *cut* the green things off, or do you *pull* the green things off? I had to call my mother up and ask her what to do with strawberries. She gave me a whole lot of chatter, but you think she knew? Some authority. If I told *you* I didn't know what to do with strawberries, you'd start sobbing, you'd think it was so great. Or else you'd give me that holy look all night that makes me want to retch."

"So I cry in the movies," Patrick said, "put a bullet in my heart."

———

46

"Two years ago I was sixteen and I didn't even know you," Mona said, sounding very rattled. "I was sixteen years old and I was having a very good time. What did I have to meet you for? I was learning to drink beer. Every afternoon we'd all go over to the Alcove and Archie Beaufort would feed me a teaspoonful of beer. He was my boyfriend. And every once in a while he'd kiss me on the ear. I can see his big white face. That was probably the last good year I'll ever have."

"You should have married Archie Beaufort," Patrick said.

"Archie Beaufort was a goon."

Patrick tried to take her hand and she rapped his knuckles with the handle of a knife. He groaned. "There's just one thing you seem to be forgetting."

"Don't tell me, let me guess," Mona said. "You love me—yes?"

Patrick took a breath, groaned again, and went back to making circles with the glass.

"I'm sorry if I hurt your feelings," Mona said, "but it makes me nervous to hear people say that. I've been hearing it for ten thousand years. Like one time before my father died he lost all his money. More than one time, but one time in particular. And we all had to stay in one room in some ratty hotel near Forty-second Street. I slept with my mother and him. Gordon and Monroe slept—I don't know—in a shoe box on the windowsill; in a bureau drawer, like Kayo. Anyway, in the middle of the night the phone would ring and he'd get up cursing and put his clothes on and they'd fight awhile and he'd go out. And right in the middle of the action, the whole time, they'd both keep screaming, 'I love you, I love you.' And the people next door would hammer on the walls and they'd scream it out louder, 'I love you.' Especially my mother, she's very big on that."

"Did she?" Patrick asked.

"Did she love him? My father? Sure. She didn't know him from Adam, but she was all over him, like ivy. He was nice, all right. He used to shave my eyebrows."

"Off?" Patrick said in horror.

"No, no, the in-between part. I happened to be a very hairy child. My brother Gordon didn't like my father terribly well," she went on, dreamy and detached. "He liked his own father. He used to carry around a big slate with 'My father's name was Sanders Carew' written on it, until my mother made him cut it out. She thought it hurt my father's feelings, which I doubt. My father couldn't stand Gordon. He was always knocking Gordon's teeth out or whatnot, by accident. Playing baseball. Gordon detested baseball. Gordon was pretty nice about it, except for the slate."

"And what about Monroe?" Patrick said.

"Monroe's father was another father altogether," Mona said. "You know that. Those two were before my time, Gordon's father and Monroe's father."

"Did Monroe like your father?"

"I don't think so. Once he threw a roll at him."

"Holy hat," Patrick said. "It sounds awful." He was distressed. He disapproved of Mona's mother and her brothers because he thought they were not serious, but he liked them. They were gaudy—all fuss and feathers and bounce. Now they'd been jarred out of focus. They were mortal, guilty. They were strangers.

————

"I guess," Mona said. "And then she married What's-his-name, and it was more of the same, only he had lots of cash. We went to live in France for a while and it was all very chic in a downtrodden way. They planted the boys in some terrible school and What's-his-name's sousy old French aunt was supposed to keep me out of their hair. We all used to eat dinner at a big table under a chandelier made out of glass morning glories. We were about a mile away from each other. And What's-his-name would sit at one end of the table and give my mother the blast. And she'd blot herself on her napkin and give it back from the other end, the counterblast. But anyway, what I started to say, they'd both stick in all these 'I love you's'—their veins would be bulging, that didn't stop them—'I love you, I love you.' And they did. In a manner of speaking."

"What *was* his name?" Patrick asked nervously. He and Mona were strangers. There was nothing between them but a kitchen table, they had no points of reference but a candle in a clamshell apiece and a couple of cockeyed hats. It was intolerable, shameful. He didn't want to be married to this girl. He couldn't think how it had happened.

"Jacques," Mona said. "Moldy. Was he moldy! He was always leaning on me. That type." She put her forefingers on her eyelids and pressed them closed. "This world isn't set up just the way I'd have done it myself," she said, and her voice cracked. "No kidding."

"Don't cry," Patrick said. He was afraid to touch her.

"Did you ever see me cry? I never cry." She was trembling. She spread her fingers to cover her face, and Patrick looked at her hands and at her wedding ring. "The afternoon I came out here—well, here's how I happened to

---

49

come out here, I'll give you the whole gestalt: After you left for your nine o'clock class I cleaned up the apartment and I got dressed and I went to the doctor. I cut my Milton and Abnormal. I hate Abnormal anyhow."

"You went to the *doctor?*" said Patrick, all alarm. "Are you sick?"

"I'm not sick; be quiet. So then afterwards I took the subway back up to 116th Street and I went to the market and I bought some lamb chops. And I was debating whether I should go home and get rid of my lamb chops and maybe be late for my Shakespeare, or go straight to my Shakespeare and take my lamb chops with me. I was standing on the corner there pondering this big problem and waiting for the light to change. My hair was combed and I looked, you know, I looked all right. Nice. I had my navy blue suit on. Navy blue. And I started to cross the street and a man came across. He looked all right. I hardly noticed him. But then he said in some very affected voice, 'My, what an attractive girl!' So I looked down. And then, when he got right beside me, he said, right *at* me, right into my face, 'You *bum*.'" She stared at Patrick through her fingers; she looked stricken and very, very scared.

"He was drunk," Patrick said.

"No."

Patrick got up and went around to squat on the floor next to her chair. He circled her wrists with his fingers. "That guy sounds to me like nothing but a very sick person," he said gently. "But I know how you feel."

"You don't know how I feel. All this rapport junk is junk. My mother was in gorgeous rapport with every junky husband she ever had. And in the middle of her chest she thought they were crumbs."

———

"That's different," Patrick said. "We're altogether different."

"What are you holding my hand for?" Mona said crabbily. "Stop holding my hand! I'm pregnant."

"For Pete's *sake*," Patrick said. He was astounded. "Imagine that!" He let go of her abruptly and sat hard on the floor.

"Imagine that, imagine that," Mona said despondently. "I'm having a baby and it could look like you. It could scratch its head the way you do. You scratch the left side of your head with your right hand and the right side of your head with your left hand. If I have a baby and it scratches its head like that, I'll kill myself, I mean it."

"I won't do it anymore," Patrick promised.

"I *like* it. You don't understand. I was walking up Broadway and I was shaking. You don't know how bad you'd feel. I felt as if somebody'd spat on me. Somebody who knew what he was spitting on. And all of a sudden I had a feeling—I could have a little child by the hand and be walking up Broadway and all the people on Broadway would look at us and they'd have wolf's heads instead of people's heads. They'd have fangs and little flickering glittering eyes and they'd be slavering and looking at me and this child that was just the way you were when you were a little boy and ate that bark. Oh, it was awful!"

"And then what? Where was I all this time?"

"Well, that's the thing. I didn't want to go to my Shakespeare and first I thought I'd go over to the college and look for you. But you'd have been at work by then, in Admissions, and I didn't want to go there. And then I realized something I never realized before. If you saw a lot of people on Broadway, Patrick, with wolf's heads and fangs and things, you'd say to yourself, 'Goodness gracious mercy me, look at all those poor people with wolf's heads, those poor sick people, they must feel terrible about it.' And then you'd go look up the name of a specialist. You'd be very tactful and sweet about it and you wouldn't let on you'd noticed anything, but you'd get them all to the specialist. And then you'd sell your socks to pay the bill."

"I really don't think I would," Patrick said.

"Yes. It's your tragic flaw. And when they ripped off your arms and they ripped off your legs and you were just a bloody piece of meat on the pavement on Broadway, your voice that's just like Mickey Rooney's would float around in the air saying, 'Those poor, poor people, they were even sicker than I thought.'" She took one hand away from her face and clutched her throat.

"I don't sound a bit like Mickey Rooney," Patrick said resentfully.

"Moses supposes his toeses are roses," Mona said wearily, "but Moses supposes erroneously. You sound more like Mickey Rooney than Mickey Rooney does." She sighed and put her face down on her arms on the table, turned away from him so that all he got was a view of her red straw hat and the babyish downy back of her neck. "So then I called my friendly neighborhood mother," she said in a tired-out voice, "and gave her the word. She said, 'Mona! Oh, my baby,' and wept till I just about had tears running down my arm from the telephone. Then she said she'd sell a bond."

"She doesn't have to sell a bond," Patrick said. "I'll quit school."

"You would, too, you *boob*," Mona said, with no breath to spare. "You would. Don't be so boring. My father left me lots of jack and once I get my hands on it, I'll buy my mother off."

"And what about me?" Patrick said. "It's my child, too, isn't it? What about me? I'm responsible."

"Don't be so boring," Mona begged. "And that's how I happened to come out here. I wanted to look at things and think and be all by myself and not near you."

"For how long?" Patrick asked anxiously. "Not for long? Not forever?"

Mona didn't answer him. "All I can think about is how awful everything is. Take my mother. I like her quite a lot. I like her very well, to be frank with you. And I shouldn't. Old creeping Jane, she's awful. She took every one of us kids aside—Monroe, then Gordon, then me—and told every single one of us that our own particular father was the only man she ever loved. She doesn't even know the difference, Patrick. I shouldn't like her at all, don't you think? She's awful. Things are *awful,* don't you think? Take my brother Gordon, for example. He gets fruitier every minute, he wears rouge. She lifted her head and looked at him, pinched and frightened. "If I saw Gordon and I didn't know he was Gordon, I'd look at something else, so I wouldn't have to look at him. But just the same, I like him very well. And Monroe is mean, he's as mean as anything, and the trouble is, he's got a conscience. When Gordon was a baby, Monroe hated Gordon's father so much that he used to pick Gordon right up from the floor by the rims of his ears. That's how Gordon got so deaf. Monroe told me that, and he told Gordon and my mother and God knows who all, probably perfect strangers. And he hates himself for it, he flails himself for it, and do you know what? The whole time, if Gordon wasn't two feet taller than Monroe,

Monroe would still be picking him up by his ears. The whole time. And still and all, I like Monroe. A lot."

"Don't you like me anymore?" Patrick said.

"Sure I do. I never said I didn't," she said faintly. "It's just that everything's so awful, Patrick. Don't you think everything's awful?" She put her cold hands on the nape of his neck and rammed his face against the stiff, faded bodice of her bathing suit. His hat fell off. "Don't you think it's awful?" she moaned into his hair, hanging on to him and kissing his ears and his forehead in a transport of despair. "Isn't life crummy, though, isn't it low?"

"Yes," he said happily, kissing her chest, wondering if she'd broken his nose, "I guess it is. I guess it's pretty bad."

Tib's Eve

The two beds in Catherine's room in Copely Hall were
narrow cots without headboard or footboard. When she
woke in hers in the middle of the morning, the other bed,
Ticky Post's, was empty. Ticky's patent leather hatbox,
packed, was on Ticky's striped chintz chair. Ticky's new
red dress, quite smart for a size 16, hung poised against her
closet door. Ticky was pointed toward Pittsburgh.

Catherine turned her face to the wall. She was only a little sick—a feverish cold according to the doctor—but she
was very disheartened. From beyond the door to the hall
came the sounds of departure. Suitcases clunk-clunked
down the shabby stairs of the dormitory, which was a

made-over Victorian house; good-byes were shouted in the halls, and the flaming jaw of Miss Quelser, the house-mother, had been kissed and kissed and kissed again. The atmosphere was gay. Catherine, for one, was fed up with it.

Ticky Post slammed open the door, charged over the threshold, and slammed the door shut again. Catherine lay still, her eyes to the wall. Even not looking at Ticky, you could see her: toothy, with black bangs.

"Well," Ticky said, tight-lipped, "are you going to speak, or not?"

Catherine turned her head, but very slowly. Ticky, who was aged fourteen and a half to Catherine's thirteen, wore a trollopy housecoat and silver mules. "Sure," Catherine said. "What'd you like to hear me say?"

"Ask me if I stole your watch," Ticky urged. "Go ahead, ask me." She shucked off her housecoat and began to dredge herself with powder from a box of Follow Me. "Don't look!" she said to Catherine.

"I never said you stole my watch," Catherine said, in a voice that was worn and conspicuously bored. "I merely said it was stolen. My father sent it one week ago today, *n'est-ce pas?* On my birthday. I kept it right on my bureau. Too ugly to wear and too expensive to throw away, *n'est-ce pas?* And yesterday it was gone. *Ergo,* it was stolen. By somebody."

"Don't *look,* I said."

Catherine groaned and flopped over on her side, her pointed, cranky face confronting the cold tan wall. "I just hope you realize that my true-blue mother will plotz."

"You should've thought about your mother before you pushed Gloria Mulligan out that window," Ticky said. "If

———

it was my mother, that's what she'd plotz about, not because I lost some mere watch."

"I didn't lose it, it was swiped," Catherine said. "And my true-blue mother's a materialist. I could've chopped up Gloria Mulligan and stoked a furnace with her, and my true-blue mother wouldn't turn a hair."

"If that's so, then I feel sorry for you," Ticky said. She peered worriedly over her shoulder, inspecting her powdery backside. "Gloria's ankle's green as grass. Quelser's furious. Listen, do you think I have a very big butt?"

"How can I tell you unless I look?" Catherine grumbled. Very briefly, she looked. "Geez, Lou-*ise!*" she said. "Yes." She thought Ticky looked like something out of *National Geographic* and considered telling her so, but, for some reason, forbore.

Ticky was well on her side of the line. The line, meticulously drawn in chalk, and frequently renewed, divided the little room into halves. Ticky's territory was neatly kept; Catherine's was a mess. Ticky began to put on her clothes, particularly a flighty red hat with a nose veil.

"I feel sorry for a person whose mother lets them wear that hat," Catherine said.

Ticky ignored her. She plumped herself down on her bed with a lipstick, a brush, and a mirror. Suddenly, artfully, she had an upper lip.

"You look more like a fish than anybody I ever knew in my whole life," Catherine said. "A great big mackerel with bangs. And socks in its brassiere." She sat up, cross-legged, draping her brown blanket over her head so that a flap hung down across her brow, and bundling the rest around her shoulders. "Do I look like Moondog?"

Ticky gave her full attention to her lower lip.

"Never mind," Catherine said. "I do look like Moon-dog, though." She got out of bed and, with her blanket around her, dragged herself over to her bureau mirror to be sure. Her thick, mismanaged hair, tea-colored except for a badly bleached skunklock, poked out from under her hood. She looked a lot like Moondog, and she felt terrible. She flared her nostrils at a bottle of medicine left by the doctor. Then she went back to her bed and lay down on it.

"They're going to boot me," she said, almost in tears. "Even if my mother did go to school here. There's no sentiment in this crowd."

"*Quel dommage*," Ticky said. She licked her right thumb and used it to straighten the seams of her stockings.

"You're all heart, Ticky, old bean," Catherine said. "You know that?"

"You've been looking for it," Ticky said tensely. She dropped her lipstick, and, to Catherine's surprise, instead of picking it up, kicked it under her bed. "You think you're such a bullet! First you practically murder Gloria Mulligan. Then you go around saying your watch is stolen. You're a maniac."

"The only ones I told my watch was stolen are the suspects," Catherine said, in a reasonable tone.

"I'm not a suspect! Go tell Miss Quelser your watch was stolen. She'll never believe it."

"Naturally she won't," said Catherine. "I know that. Of course she won't. She thinks I'm depraved. She thinks I haven't got all my marbles. But don't even worry about it, chesty. Just throw another log on the fire. Just stuff another sock in your brassiere."

Ticky stood in the middle of the room, lumpy and nervous

---

in her new red dress. "Listen, Catherine, I didn't take it."

Catherine looked sidewise at her. She was convinced that Ticky had nothing to do with the missing watch, but she couldn't, for reasons she didn't know, bring herself to tell Ticky that. She shut her eyes. "How are the hock shops in P-burgh, old bean? Do a big trade in hot watches?"

Ticky made a strangling noise, picked up her hatbox, and fled, leaving the door open.

Catherine got up at once. She closed the door carefully. Then she collected an armful of books from her bookcase and climbed back into bed with them. She could hear, outside, the slamming of car doors, and the last cheerful leave-takings. She arranged the books on top of her, like rocks on a lonely grave. Finally, the house was quiet. After a few minutes Cooley, the gimpy old janitor, went down the hall past her room, on some errand. "*Man*-on-the-floor," he chanted, as he was made to do. "*Man*-on-the-floor."

·   ·   ·

Copely Hall had been, since before Catherine's mother's time, an off-campus dormitory of the Copely School for Girls, an establishment that Catherine chose to think of, in two senses, as a bad girls' school. The dormitory had its own kitchen and dining room and was full of the stale smells of green soap and cream sauce. Its downstairs sitting rooms were crowded with snake plants, hat racks, stopped clocks, and balding mohair sofas. Catherine was a career misfit. She had a broad experience of schools and dormitories, but she had never felt so close to the end of the line as she did now after only six months at Copely. She lay with one arm across her eyes. After Copely Hall, what?

Pushing the books aside, she closed her eyes, put her fingers in her ears, and prayed. In a little while she slept.

When she woke, the room was dim and chill, and in a house across the way the lights were on. It was almost suppertime. The radiator in her room made a wheezy clang. Presently, there was a knock at the door. Catherine said, "Now what?" and the door swung open and Cooley, the janitor, stood there, with a crockery plate in one hand, a monkey wrench in the other, and a scarlet carnation through a buttonhole of his shirt. He had a crest of stiff white hair, like a prophet or a cockatoo. Cooley smiled—a smile that seemed to Catherine unwarrantedly festive. He saluted her with the wrench.

"What's the matter?" she said edgily.

"Nothing I know of," Cooley said, limping in. "Excepting for the radiator, and that I've come to fix." He put the plate on her desk and switched on her old goosenecked student lamp. Its shade turned luminously green and lovely, and Catherine sat up against the icy wall, the blanket pulled around her.

Cooley picked up the plate and set it on the bump of her knees. "Eat that," he said, retreating. On the plate was an enormous wedge of chocolate cake.

"Where'd you get that?" Catherine said, squinting at it.

"I got it," he said. "Eat it. You know what you'll be getting for your supper. A crust of bread and the scrapings of tin."

"What you say is true," Catherine said. She could see the tray Miss Quelser would send her—tomato soup, lukewarm, a horrible, shuddery red. She was hungry for the chocolate cake, and she ate it, icing last. It was delicious. Cooley stood watching her with his monkey wrench laid over his heart, next to the carnation. He was looking very spruce—more so than he ought to, Catherine thought.

"Where'd you get the weed?" she said nervously.

"Ah," he said. "That's for you." He advanced and laid the flower across the empty plate.

"Thank you very much," Catherine said, easing the blanket up under her chin. "Listen, is everybody gone?"

"Lost, gone, stolen, strayed, or blown away with the wind," Cooley said happily. He sat down on the foot of her bed. "You're Helen Gerrity's daughter. I'd know you by her eyes. I've been looking for a word with you."

"Did you know her?" Catherine said. "My mother?"

"I did," he said. "Her lovely eyes. As black as Cromwell's heart. You wouldn't see the like of them in twelve months of Sundays." He got up from Catherine's bed and moved over to the radiator. His bad leg gave him a syncopated gait, like a man half minded to break into a jig. Lowering himself by the radiator, he stared at it sourly.

"Listen, Cooley—Mr. Cooley," Catherine said. "Are you sure you feel like fixing that radiator this exact minute? Because it's been broken forever, so why bother?"

Cooley paid no attention to her. He was twisting a valve. "Have you found your watch?" he asked.

Her spine went stiff. "How'd you know about that? Does Miss Quelser know?"

"No," he said. "And not likely to."

"That's all I need," Catherine said. "All I have to do is make a simple statement like 'Miss Quelser, somebody clipped my watch' and she puts the spit on me. I'm a troublemaker, in case you didn't know it. She's only told me that around a million times. I'm a troublemaker, and I pushed Gloria Mulligan out the window." She put her bare feet on the floor and sat on the edge of the bed, hunched under her blanket and scowling.

"Did you now? Push her?" Cooley asked interestedly. "Was she kilt?"

"Now listen," Catherine said. "I heard you talking to her. Yesterday. So you know she wasn't."

"Ah," Cooley said. He smiled a little.

"All that happened was that she was sitting on the windowsill in her room, moaning," Catherine said. "She's a moaner. She's always *moaning*. She got a B in Civilization, or some repulsive, tragic thing. And I was talking to her roommate, who happens to be Allison Dickman. And Gloria, who happens to be very high-strung, was interrupting us. Moaning. And finally I sort of opened the window. And I said, 'Gloria, jump out the window, will you?' That's all I said. And the big stupid bonehead jumped. Nobody has a right to be that high-strung. Am I right?"

"Is Allison that one with the twisty nose?"

"It's not so twisty," Catherine said. "It's quite piquant, if you look at it right. I mean, like sideways." She showed him how to look at it—turning her profile and squashing up her nose with the tip of her finger. Cooley seemed doubtful. "If you get a chance," Catherine said, "maybe you'll casually remark that it's piquant. Okay? Where she can hear you." Cooley nodded solemnly.

"There was a roof right underneath," Catherine went on. "She turned her fat ankle, that's all. Gloria! A seven-foot warthog that never takes a bath. Allison hates her. I never laid a hand on her, I swear it."

Cooley raised his wrench and made a tiny, tentative adjustment of its jaws. "Is she a friend of yours, this Allison?"

Tib's Eve

"No," Catherine said, looking down at her bare, dingy feet. "And that's not true about Gloria not taking baths, either. She takes more baths than I do." She glanced at Cooley, who was leaning back against the radiator. "Allison has a very fine character," Catherine said. "Like she's always finding good in people. She loves every single person she ever met in her life. She loves Gloria because Gloria's very fond of animals and polite to her mother and all that." Cooley didn't appear to be impressed. "I didn't exactly push her," Catherine said bleakly. "Maybe I nudged her a little. That's pretty awful, isn't it?"

"Hmm?" Cooley said, rousing. "Indeed it is. A terrible thing. She does nothing but whinge, though, that Mulligan one."

"That's no reason to push somebody out a *window,*" Catherine said. "She didn't even tell on me. You know who told? Allison told." Catherine chewed on the end of her thumb. "I really racked up around here. And then my watch was pinched, and they're going to pitch me out of here. My true-blue parents will cream me."

"Will your mother be taking it hard?" Cooley asked.

"I really don't know," Catherine said. She got up and moved over to the desk chair, still wrapped in her blanket. She sat down facing the back of the chair, with her chin resting on the crossbar, and watched Cooley tinker indecisively with a piece of dismantled radiator. "I couldn't care less," she said. "My mother burns me, anyway. It's my father I'm worried about. They'll have to send him to a hernia sanatorium."

"What's your father up to now?" Cooley asked. He sounded suspicious.

63

"He's a big door man," Catherine said indifferently.

"A doorman!" Cooley said. He was scandalized. "Who'd believe it?"

"Not like that. He's a big man in steel doors. He's a steel-door tycoon."

"I knew that fella when him and her was courting," Cooley said. "I never liked the look of him. She married him out of here. She was only a bit of a girl like yourself. A year or two older. Did you know that?"

Catherine was a little shocked. "I don't know if I knew it or not. My father's very nice." Cooley regarded her stolidly. "He sent me that watch for my birthday," she said. "Or rather his secretary did. But he told her to. My mother never sent me a thing."

"Wouldn't it be from the both of them?"

"Well . . . maybe. But I never like anything she sends me. When she sends me anything, I always tell her I hate it."

"Why is that?" said Cooley, frowning at her.

"Because she burns me," Catherine said patiently. "All she ever sends me is poetry books, anyway." Trailing her blanket, she went over to the bed and brought back one of the books that lay there. She held it out to Cooley, who looked it over thoroughly but didn't touch it. "She happens to think that poetry is the biggest thing since sex," Catherine said. She put the book down on the desk and then went back to her chair. "I write poetry myself," she said. " 'The worm at the heart of the rose'—you think that's a good image?" Cooley appeared to be thinking it over. "I have a poem about that," Catherine said. "And I have one about a bug-eaten half shell at the mouth of the Nile. And one about my heart is a festering sore. Those are my best ones."

"I never liked the look of that fella," Cooley said stubbornly. "As wide acrost the shoulders as a herring between the eyes. 'Yes, ma'am' and 'No, ma'am' and 'Ma'am, if you please.' She could of done better than a spindleshanks like him."

"You wait'll they bounce me out of here," Catherine said, with a hollow laugh. "Wait'll she finds out my watch was stolen. It'll be gala. My father'll sit around like I kicked him in the stomach. He'll bleed all over me, but he won't *say* anything. But she'll go through the roof—psst-boom!—like a rocket."

"Is she still light-fingered herself?" Cooley said.

"Still what?"

"Yes, sir," Cooley said. He was full of admiration. "She'd steal the eye out of your head and you looking at her."

"My *mother?*" Catherine said.

"Yes, sir," Cooley said.

"Why?" Catherine said, astonished. "Are you sure? You mean she took things? Why?" She held on to the back of the chair and stared at him.

"Nothing—only divilment," Cooley said. "There was a sly one here name of Juney. She had handfuls of money, Juney, and she never left off flashing it. Well, one night Helen snicked it off her. Next day Juney threw a fit, but they couldn't find who done it. And then by and by Juney gets a certain letter in the mail. So this letter, you see, is from overseas, from some Italian orphans' home—a worthy institution. It's all about the poor babies with their pure hearts and innocent lips praying like sixty to the Blessed Mother—and all for Juney. And thank you for the glorious donation,

---

which has purchased a church bench and bread. What a yell and holler! Juney near died. She was a Lutheran, to add to her troubles."

"Wasn't that a little mean, don't you think?" Catherine said. She didn't think it was mean, particularly—just not terribly moral.

"Mean on who? On Juney? No. First off, she had a bad character. And second of all, the balls of her legs was turned to the front. There was neither shape nor make to her."

"So what happened to my mother when they caught her?"

"Divil they caught. They never caught her. We had a housemother then, old Finster, a mountain of flesh with a cast in her eye. When something queer was going on, she'd line them up in the midst of them snake bushes and throw them a look from that herring eye. The sweat would break on them. But Helen never faltered."

"Did she do it for spite?" Catherine said. She hooked her bare feet on the rungs of the chair, puzzled and uneasy.

"Spite wasn't in her," Cooley said. "She was happy as Larry—rampageous. Holy Father, she shouldn't have married that fella. I could have told her that. She was meant for something big."

"Like what?" Catherine said, drearily scratching her neck. "Bank jobs?"

"Ah, listen, can't you? You're nearly as thick as your father."

"Let's get down to the bare bone on this," Catherine said gruffly. "Are you sure this person was my mother?"

"Well, it was and it wasn't." Cooley laughed. "God knows she wasn't your mother then."

"She was always my mother," Catherine said. "She just wasn't my mother *yet*."

"You're somebody's mother yourself then, for all we know, and somebody's granny and great-granny. And great-great-granny," Cooley said. "It's a wonder to me you've time to clean your teeth."

"I am not," Catherine said. It was a frightening thought. She had no strong objection to being somebody's mother, but not full-time. Phantom children and grandchildren and great-great-grandchildren crowded her, draining her of identity. "I'm just a person on Social Probation," she said. The sudden sense of her mother's existence—real, separate, private—affected her queerly. "Was she prettier than me?"

"Some," Cooley said.

"I guess you liked her."

"I did," he said. "She was a girl and a half."

Catherine examined the webs between her thumbs and forefingers. The right web had a little nick in it. She'd heard a theory that if you got a cut there, you died of lockjaw. It was probably a lie, though. "I used to like her," Catherine said. "At one time."

Cooley pointed his wrench at her bare feet. "You'd think that fella'd buy you some shoes," he said.

Tears of self-pity came to her eyes, although she had never suffered from a lack of shoes. "When I was a little bit of a child, my mother got a big bang out of me," she told him. "I used to run up to her in Washington Square Park with a big bunch of dopey leaves and I'd say, 'Aren't they beautiful?' and she'd say, 'Aren't *you* beautiful?' and she'd kiss me, and all that. I was in like Flynn in those days. But that was a long time ago." The corners of her mouth were

---

turned down, and her eyes were wet. "She's not at all like that now. You wouldn't like her. She only cares about parties and fooling around. That's *all*. She's always flouncing around with a drink in her hand and her back all bare and her feet hanging out of her shoes. She's always *laughing*. That woman laughs twenty-four hours a day, Cooley—what's so funny, I'd like to know. She calls everybody 'darling' but my father. She calls the elevator man 'darling,' Cooley. How'd you like it if your mother went around calling the elevator man 'darling'? You wouldn't like it."

Cooley shifted his position on the floor. "Well," he said uneasily, "I don't know as I'd object."

"You wouldn't like it. How'd you like it if every time your dumb old man said 'boo,' your mother creamed him? All right, he's a moaner—you think Gloria moans, you should meet my father—but she shouldn't treat him like that. It isn't nice." She glared at Cooley, who was sitting still, with his eyes cast down. "Is it?"

"If it was me married on him, I'd stick a pin in his navel and give it out that he died of the shortness of breath," Cooley said glumly.

"Listen, Cooley," Catherine said. "One time she was having a party and I was helping out in the kitchen. And this horrible man my mother knows called Buggy Foch came in and started playing rich-man-poor-man on the buttons of my blouse. I don't appreciate that stuff. And I couldn't make him go away. And I hit him with the dishrag, and I went to find my mother, and you know what she said? I was *crying*. He made me *cry*. She said, 'Get back in the kitchen and behave yourself. Don't you dare spoil my party.'" Catherine hitched up a corner of her blanket and scrubbed her moist eyes with it.

———

"Poor child," Cooley said, looking up at her.

"Don't sit on the floor, Cooley," Catherine said. "Sit on a chair, for goodness' sake. Thank you for that cake. It was delicious." She shoved out Ticky's chair for him, and he entrusted himself to its striped chintz lap, his big hands balanced neatly on his knees. Catherine sat down on the bed across from him, hopelessly tangled in her blanket. "Thank you for the flower."

"Poor Helen," Cooley said. "It was that fella she married. I wouldn't give a tin whistle for him. But she was that gone on him. You'd have thought he was somebody, the carry-on she made."

"If she wants to be such a hotshot lady, she should be one—right? She shouldn't laugh so much and mouse around with Buggy Foch. When they called her up about Gloria, they made me talk to her. She said, 'Darling, did you push that little girl out the window?' My own *mother* asked me that. I said, 'What do you think?' She cried like a fountain. And you should hear what she tells Buggy Foch on the telephone. I listened on the extension plenty of times."

"Sure, all of that has nothing to do with you," Cooley said.

"She's my *mother*."

"That's neither her fault nor yours," Cooley said. "It's a circumstance."

Catherine hesitated before she spoke, a few tears sliding off the end of her chin. Cooley's point of view seemed to her a highly original one. "Would you like a drink?" she said abruptly. "I happen to have some liquor very handy." She went over to her cluttered bureau. On it, in the middle of a lot of furry dust, were a wad of cellophane, gummy with orange icing, a contraband package of Kools, the bottle of medicine, an old toy tiger wearing a green felt hat, and a single dirty glass.

Catherine took the glass down the hall to the shower room. There she washed it. Then she returned with the clean glass and a paper cup, which she set down on the bureau. "That's Paddy," she said, pointing to the toy tiger. "My mother gave me him a long time ago, when I still used to like her. I used to be crazy about him when I was a child." She dug a bottle of what purported to be Halo shampoo out of her top drawer and uncapped it. "This is really peach brandy. It's for cramps." Cooley nodded his approval. She poured a little of the brandy into the paper cup and a great deal into the glass. She took the glass over to Cooley. "Do you really think she used to like him quite a lot?"

"She did," Cooley said. "She thought the sun rose for his pleasure."

"Boy," Catherine said. "Did she miss the boat." She raised her paper cup obligingly. "Here's looking up your address."

"Mother of God," Cooley said. "Would you call that a toast." He leaned over and touched his glass to the rim of Catherine's paper cup. "I'm about to give you a proper toast." He coughed, formally. "The lake is not encumbered by the swan. Nor the steed by the bridle. Nor the sheep by the wool. Nor the man by the heart that is in him." He looked at her and took a swallow from his glass. Catherine took a tiny, burning sip from her paper cup.

"I think that's beautiful," she said. "Is it supposed to be true?"

"Listen till I tell you," Cooley said. "Whether it's true or it's not true, it's a hell of a lot better than 'Here's looking up your address.'"

"Do you happen to know a toast about people not getting thrown out of school, and all that?" Catherine asked. "For instance, everything working out for the best, and everybody doing what they're supposed to, and Gloria not getting gangrene in her ankle? Like 'Cheers.' Or 'Happy days.' Only not those."

He raised his glass again. "To Tib's Eve," he said gravely.

"When's Tib's Eve?"

"You don't know? Your mother would know. It's neither before nor after Easter."

"You mean it's *never*—like the second Tuesday of next week? *Never?*"

"I wouldn't want to put it just like that. I'd say it was sometime. Or never, at the furthest." For a moment or two he studied Catherine across her paper cup and then, startlingly, he winked at her. After they drank, they both looked at the Halo bottle, but it was empty. Cooley got slowly to his feet. "I'm as stiff as Paddy's father when he was nine months dead," he said good-humoredly.

"That's Paddy," Catherine said, nodding toward the toy tiger on the bureau.

"So it is," Cooley said. "I'd know him in a crowd." He put his glass down on Catherine's desk.

"Let me ask you something," Catherine said. She was a little dizzy from the brandy. She sighted along the seam in her empty paper cup. "Do you think people are supposed to love one another? I mean, I don't like to be corny, but that's what my mother always said."

"They are if they're able, but not if they're not," Cooley

———

said. It sounded pretty obvious, the way he said it. He'd been backing toward the radiator, which was clanking again, but now he changed course and, picking up his wrench, headed for the door. "Marconi himself couldn't fix that thing," he said. "And I haven't the proper wrench for the job." He went out, closing the door firmly behind him.

Catherine dropped the blanket on the floor. In her too small, not very clean pajamas, she walked over to the bed and took the carnation from the plate the cake had been on and put it in the empty Halo bottle. She licked her finger and mopped up all the cake crumbs and ate them. After that she lay down on the bed, with Paddy on her chest. She looked straight into his knowing green glass eyes. She smoothed a kink in his tail and flicked his meager whiskers. Then she set his cap straight, and her watch fell out of it.

———

The
Solution
to Canned
Peas

"Let's look on the sunny side," Margaret says, in the twinkly, flirty, aren't-I-awful, suffering way that maddens him. "If our daughter does murder me, you can pick up the threads with that girl from Chicago."

"I could hit you with a brick when you go into that routine," Brendan says. "Stay focused. Where did you find this notebook again?"

"Oh, you know. Around. In her room. I'm freezing." She stamps her feet and slaps her hands together. Wet and breathless, red-faced and half-blinded in steamy spectacles, they have been shoveling snow in the dark and enjoying it, but they are back now in the orderly, bright kitchen, disrupting its air of professional calm. "You blew on my fingers to warm them," she says. "When we lived in that rattrap in Buffalo."

"Toes," he says. "Also toes. Also other body parts." He grasps her fingers, but she pulls them away. "*Where* in her room, Margaret? I know you, you're a Sherlock, you're a snoop. Is there anything sweet in this house?"

"To eat, you mean. No. We're dieting, the girls and I. And Betty Crocker doesn't live here anymore. When the girl from Chicago moved in, Betty Crocker took early retirement." She gives a few bye-bye hand flaps to the copper pots overhead, the double ovens, the marble pastry stone set into the pretty maple counters.

"Margaret, I could run you through the chipper when you get like this. Months go by and not a word out of you, then suddenly, splat! I'm a bum again. How much am I expected to put up with?"

"Plenty," says Margaret, grinning and twinkling. "Herbal tea? Decaf? Ersatz cocoa or diet soda, which? Them's the libations I can offer you. None of them terrific, but none of them poisoned. What does it matter where the notebook was? I found it and it's something we need to have a talk about. Imitation cocoa, I think. But I'll float a marshmallow because when all is said and done, I'm a decent sort."

"I don't want to have a talk," Brendan says. "Where are they, the girls?"

"Your eldest daughter is up at West Point. Lying down for soldiers, unless I miss my guess. Your next eldest is skiing with a boy I hate the looks of but have insufficient evidence to indict. Your twins—this is chronological order,

I'm not prioritizing here—your twins are tap dancing. In keeping with their awful life's ambition to stay adorable forever. One of them has taken up with some shifty kid. The little one is at a sleepover with Priscilla and Nonny. Nonny's mama is an alky."

"Priscilla's the tartlet, am I right? And Nonny's the milk truck? They're okay, aren't they? Nice girls and so forth?"

"Nice girls, sure. If you'd played your sperms right, we could have had nice boys and my hands wouldn't tremble nor my eyelid twitch. Maybe I'd still get into an eight."

"If we'd of had nice boys," Brendan says, sucking up cocoa in a noisy way forbidden by his daughters, "they'd be drugged off their ass or quadriplegics from football practice. Or dressing up in ladies' clothing."

"I guess so. Life is a sitcom. Life is a tabloid headline. Why don't you want to talk with me, Brennie? When did that come on you?"

"Talk to you I can do. Have a talk, no. You make all these categories of talks and dialogues. Long talk. Good talk. Serious talk. Frank. Family. Heartfelt. I did that already and it didn't work out. We used to be married, we had knockdown drag-outs. Then all of a sudden we had this thing called 'a marriage' and we're into heartfelts and meaningfuls. It's like 'a marriage' is sitting in that chair between us, wanting to have 'a talk.' " He gives the chair a kick with his big bare foot. "A goony-looking thing with old seaweed hanging on it like in *Popeye*."

"We were married until you cheated on me and then we had 'a marriage,' " Margaret says, drifting into the laundry room and out again. "Necessitating many a talk. Heartfelt and otherwise."

———

Suddenly he dips and flinches as a missile sails past his head. "*What in Christ?*"

"Dry socks," Margaret says, retrieving the gray woolly balls. "Were you expecting a grenade?"

"Do you think the little one's in some kind of trouble, Margie? I mean, I know it's nothing, but could her maybe leaving this notebook around so's you'd see it be some kind of, I don't know what, a signal?"

"A cry for help? Isn't that what they call it these days?"

"Stop asking me what they call things these days. Like you're a member of some secret tribe that don't know a stick is to hit someone with. Where is this notebook? I want a look at it."

"I kept it in the dishwasher hoping you'd show up and then when you didn't and she was due from school, I put it back where I got it, but it's not there now. She moved it."

"Why didn't you come out and ask her about it?"

With a groan she sinks to the floor at his feet. Literally at his feet, for she takes one of his feet up and studies it. "Red flat flippers like a beat cop's," she says. "Like my father's." She begins to work a sock on over his toes. "One little piggy went to market," she says. "Other, dumber, little piggy stayed home."

"Am I getting so I look like a cop?" Brendan says. "Guy says to me in Grand Central, I'd asked him for a light, he says, 'I'm *clean!*' Remember the time your old man smacked me on the soles with his billy? I was sleeping on your mother's couch, the one nobody had ever seen because it was covered with two slipcovers to keep it nice for when she had a home of her own?"

"I remember that my mother died on that couch," Margaret says. "On top of two slipcovers."

"Your father wanted me on the cops," Brendan says. "Nice steady job with a uniform and a pension. And a gun. I'd of been retired now."

"It was the FBI he wanted you in. But you had to have a law degree then, I think, or accounting. I notice we both look like old Irish cops lately. Not old-old. Getting there."

"Humpty and Dumpty."

"Humpty was also Dumpty, you dullard. Do all men who travel on business fool around?"

"Largely. Not since the plague, maybe. Not so much. It's pretty boring to sit in a hotel room night after night. In your drawers. Bottle of scotch for company, filling out vouchers, your expense account, call reports. These things happen. Client orders up some girls, or *you* order up some girls because the client indicates that would be appropriate. Or there are girls; you know, you run into girls. What can you say, 'I'm a daily communicant, miss, no thank you'? I have a bad enough reputation at the place, being pussy-whipped."

"We've been over this a million times," she says. "It would have been criminal to relocate over and over. Drag five little girls all over this country and all over the world on the chance of building your career in a business you don't much like anyway."

"I'd have looked a whole lot better than I do today, job security–speaking. Put the other sock on, bite my corn, whatever it is you have in mind there, Margaret. I remind you we have one kid in college, four more to come, and I don't think I'm long for this world at the place. Roggit is grouching around that I'm not a team player, plus he told Gus I don't really like clients. It's not enough the client says, 'Shit,' I say, 'Where and how much?' On top of that

I've got to hug and kiss the ugly buggers."

"Was the girl from Chicago one you ordered up? Or one that was ordered up for you?"

"I could knock your brains out, Margaret. I could sink one of your fifty-dollar knives in your pleural cavity. You know she wasn't. You know she was as clean a woman as you are yourself. Give me that fucking sock before I stuff it in your craw."

"Why do you put her in the past tense, though? Is she dead? Did she die because you parted? Why won't you tell me where you met her or what she did for a living, even? Why don't you tell me 'this was different'?" Tenderly, she tries to dress his stiffened foot with the gray, unyielding sock.

"You want to get these things in your mouth so you can go over them and over them and kill them. Kill it. Kill her." He burrows around in his spirit, seeking the solace of his feelings for the girl from Chicago, a plain, quiet, melancholy girl with pretty clothes and a plausible odd way of looking at things. But the girl, with her flawless dense skin, alive with glimpses of green and violet shadow, is a shameless girl, a fickle and a wise one. She has already found another lover and moved with him to Hawaii. Hawaii. A cartoon place in Brendan's mind. Poi and palm trees. Surfers. Ukulele music. Pineapples. He shudders to think what Margaret could do with Hawaii.

"It was in her closet on her shelf," Margaret says. "In a box fitted into another box, like a false bottom. Under a slew of baby pictures and our wedding album and some reels of home movies. What she wants with that junk I don't know."

"Christ, Margaret, do you shake down their cells every day?"

"It's my job."

"I thought the bookstore was your job. I thought the bookstore, which you hardly ever open, I might add, was supposed to be a profit center."

"It's not what I had in mind. I wanted a fireplace and good coffee and interesting customers and *books*. I've got mugs and tee shirts and greeting cards and illiterates."

"The bookstore is history; we're dumping it. Go back to PR. You were good at that. Go in with your sister Cecelia, stencil strawberries on stuff, something. Take your mind off. Pull your weight."

"Weight? I've spent all of my adult life in ditsy occupations. And/or locked up tight with five little girls, no two of whom have ever in my memory been happy at the same time. Or even healthy at the same time. I haven't hated it exactly. But it's been hard. Maybe it's me. I've found it hard. And you've been having it off or getting it on or making out or whatever the hell they call it these days. And now my littlest kid wants to kill me."

"Bullshit."

"Of course it's bullshit. I hope."

"It's just getting her anger out or whatever they call it these days," Brendan says. "Get up and I'll make us a drink. Is there anything to drink? There isn't anything to drink. Shit. My father lived to ninety on brisket and bourbon and I can't have butter on my muffin. I'm shoveling snow and I'm liking it and at the same time I'm running through this inventory of guys my age who shoveled snow and fell over and were never heard from. She doesn't want to hurt you. This is the kid in the flamingo costume in the Halloween parade. This is the kid with the squint and all the teeth who turned out cute who takes trombone. It's a phase or whatever they're calling it. Little girls are mean, they're like attack dogs."

"Remember the time she cut two thousand dollars' worth of wire off her teeth with the poultry shears?"

"Like it was yesterday. I was in, where was I? Detroit."

"You were in Chicago."

"Ah."

"When I was her age, I had a notebook I was keeping for my hope chest. I wrote this classy backhand I had copied from a nun, a terrible old Tartar, but I loved her. I had recipes. 'The Solution to Canned Peas.' "

"The solution to canned peas is to forget about canned peas."

"Would that it were so easy. Sauté some scallions, I think it was. Chop up lettuce. Sugar. God knows what all. 'The Solution to Canned Peas.' It's still canned peas, who knew that? They don't tell you that. Your daughter has hand-writing like a maniac."

"They all do. When the nuns went, there went penman-ship."

"Wednesday night a carful of kids shot out the storm door. Beebees. Maybe it was a tribute to the twins—kids the little one's age can't *drive*. But boys just follow her. Follow her home, anywhere. 'Boys just seem to follow you,' I said to her. 'So?' she said. 'I happen to have a great body.' "

"She's out of her mind, she's built like Dwight Gooden."

"Not exactly like him. Not enough like him. Quarts of boys. I irritate her. I have too much control of her environ-ment. Those are quotes."

"Are you bashing out at her?"

"Boys sending her roses in the seventh grade. Florist roses. In the seventh grade I had two Ralston boxes and a piece of string. My best friend and I talked between the buildings on the Ralston telephone. I think she was my friend because I could reach her by Ralston box. Now my youngest kid has a notebook."

"I had a notebook in the seventh grade," Brendan says, "around there. I pasted in the last frame of *Dick Tracy*. It was for Crime Fighters, Crime Busters. Told you how to dust for fingerprints."

"That may come in handy."

"Margaret, I could slaughter you for talking like that. This is some innocent kid thing, some book she thinks she's writing, some mystery plot, some game."

"That I know. It's just a kid thing. I mean, probably it is, of course it is. But one to a page: 'Bang head with poker, blame intruder'—*intruder* spelled with two *t*'s. 'Spray food with Raid. Yuck ick.' "

" 'Yuck ick' is you or her?"

"Her. 'Gross' comes into it, too. Editorially."

"It's probably some offshoot of Dungeons and Dragons."

" 'Push in front of bus.' "

"Jesus," he says. For he remembers one Saturday when his hand rose and faltered and finally snatched Margaret from the vast bloated wheels of a semi backing up behind a supermarket. It's not the same as pushing her, he thinks, not altogether; at the time his love for the Chicago girl had been at its most joyous and anguishing.

" 'Trip on stairs,' " says Margaret. " 'Torch premises.' How she spells *premises,* I leave you to surmise."

"Torch premises," he says. "Good night, this house is worth a lot of money."

Margaret snorts. " 'Soak towel Clorox. Soak towel ammonia. Wrap head in towels. Gas.' "

———

"See? See? That's pure kid crap."

"I'm not so sure it wouldn't work. They do make a poison together; it's on the labels sometimes."

"Clear your sinuses, anyway."

"Maybe you could go over to the client side, Brendan. If you feel the place is treating you like some back number."

"Maybe, I'm not sanguine. Should you call some official person, the guidance counselor or somebody? Not that I think it's worth making an issue of."

"She'd never forgive me."

"Should you talk to her? Should I?"

"Could you?"

He thinks awhile and starts to bluster, then he says, "Not on your life."

"Neither could I. I'd rather have her wrap my head in gas."

"I could kill you when you talk like that."

"Join the throng. Listen. There are Fig Newtons stashed in the freezer. Fiber, you know. Want them?"

"*Great*. Really *great*."

"Not so much enthusiasm, please. You sound deranged." She struggles, but she cannot rise. "I'm stuck. I'm stiff from shoveling. God, I dread tomorrow."

He hauls her up and onto his lap, clamping her there with his leg, imprisoning her arms.

"I'll never get over you doing this," Margaret says, looking into his eyes. "Not with the best will in the world. And I know you know that. And I know that it was worth it to you, just the same."

He feels a dislodgment in himself, a shift in his will and affections, weary, grudging, and voluptuous.

"The girl that's worried you so much, she's out of it,

she's married," Brendan says. "She lives with her husband in Hawaii." He waits, but his wife says nothing. "You know, Margaret, 'Ma and Pa Kettle Visit Waikiki,'" he says. Margaret says nothing. "She's an archivist," he says. "I met her at the client in the ordinary way of business." He waits for Margaret to say something.

"I'm an irritating woman," Margaret says. "It's hard to realize that on the whole you're even more irritating than you are irritated."

"Don't say anything about the little one, right?" Brendan says. "Don't network it, it's nothing, it'll all blow over. Nobody needs to know but me and you. Someday we'll laugh about it, right? Me and you."

"Me-um and you-um," Margaret says. "As Little Beaver used to say to big Red Ryder. Safe in the Painted Valley." She gives him a grim, flirtatious look and jigs so she rubs against him.

"Canned peas," he says, shaking his head as he dumps her to the floor. "Let's hit the Jacuzzi, Margie. Let's mess around before they all come home and catch us. Come on," he says. "Cheer up, Margaret, before I knock your block off."

He knows what she will do and say, how she'll respond to him. He expects to see her raise her hands, rippling them in the hula move; he expects to see her twinkling and grinning from the floor at him. "Aloha," he expects to hear, in the chirruping voice that maddens him. "Brendan, *aloha*."

But, to break his heart, she lies just as he dumped her. She doesn't do or say anything at all.

———

Slim Young Woman in No Distress

"'The person I know with the best sense of humor is my cat,'" Bravo said in his disconcerting whiskey tenor. "That is the first sentence."

"That's not half bad for openers," his mother, Glover, said from her drawing board. She was drawing a pith helmet and drinking Christian Brothers sherry from a plastic mug cast in the image and likeness of Fred Flintstone. The telephone was ringing, but neither of them paid it any mind. "There's a certain syntactical recklessness to it," Glover said, "but, on the other hand, it catches the interest. What's the second sentence?" She took a swallow from the mug and sighted at her son across its rim. He was a mournful and disordered little boy in appearance, but had lately been designated a gifted child. She could not imagine, therefore, why the person he knew with the best sense of humor was not herself. The phone stopped ringing. "I asked you what the second sentence was."

"I don't think you should speak to me in that tone of voice," Bravo said.

"Much as I appreciate these tips on child rearing you toss out, I'd like to hear the second sentence, please."

"I don't feel like I need any more sentences."

"I hope Baroness Montessori Von Summerhill sees things your way," Glover said. "It seems a little spare to me. You might enlarge a little on the theme. Include a few examples of McGonigle's snappy patter, witty chatter, scintillating repartee."

"Oh, please," Bravo said wearily.

"I must say, McGonigle hardly even favors me with the odd epigram," Glover said.

"You start out saying you like it and you end up not liking it one little bit. You must be a psychologically disturbed person."

"I said I liked it for openers. For openers and closers it's a touch arbitrary."

"The person I know with the best sense of humor is my cat," Bravo shouted. "And you can just take my word for it!"

"McGonigle is *my* cat," Glover said. "As a point of information. I had McGonigle before I had you."

"You didn't have *nothing* before you had me," Bravo shouted, stamping around the smart, rugless room in shoes that were not tied.

"I believe I have detected the area of your special gift,"

Glover said bitterly, drawing. "It is your destiny to extend the application of the double negative."

"Oh, please," Bravo said, letting his head loll and rolling his eyes.

"You know what I had before I had you? I had freedom. Do you know what an albatross you are? Personalities aside, do you begin to realize what it's like to have a *child* strung around your neck? Do you?"

"No," Bravo said. His voice was so muted and so effortful that she put down her Rapidograph and looked at him. He was bent double, dragging at his shoelaces. He was dirty because he refused to be washed; he was hungry because he refused to be fed; he was faced with other problems of a very considerable nature. And he was altogether incapable of tying his own shoelaces.

"Actually, Bravo," Glover said, "it's not half bad. I'm making a perfect Act of Contrition this very minute."

"What is that supposed to mean?" Bravo said, head down, hauling.

"It's religion."

"Don't start," Bravo said, clapping hands over ears.

"Ah, yes, I'd forgotten," Glover said. "You refuse to discuss religion or sex and you're rather cool to politics. Is it true that the only gifts you'll accept are flowers, books, and candy?"

"Don't start," Bravo yelled, his palms pressed tight against his ears. "Tell me when I'm older."

Glover made a broad, beckoning gesture, like a traffic cop.

"On the island?" Bravo said, dropping his hands.

"On the island. Don't jiggle anything." Glover's work area was set upon an invisible island, forbidden to Bravo except on invitation. It was a taboo he never violated. Glover shoved back from her drawing board and taboret and made a lap for Bravo. He climbed aboard her and settled his weight in a casual, impersonal way, as though she were an article of furniture. "I'd take it as a favor if you'd let me tie your shoes," she said.

Bravo burrowed his feet beneath her thigh. "I like them the way they are."

"Well, I don't like them the way they are," his mother said. "You'll break your bloody neck and then I'll have *that* to contend with." She dug out a foot and proceeded to tie a bow; very slowly, very simply, with grace and precision. She found herself engrossed in her own dexterity. "Watch," she said softly. "This way; and this way; and this way. *Et voilà.* Do you want to try the other one?" She smiled tenderly into Bravo's face—and noted that his eyes were squeezed shut. She seized his other foot by the ankle and tied the bow with dispatch. Then she thumped him on the collarbone. "You can open your eyes now. The scary part is over."

Bravo cautiously revealed to her his crystalline blue gaze. "I must have dozed off," he said, with vast hypocrisy.

"I only hope your chromosomes are spliced together right," Glover said. "I hope you didn't inherit anything."

"I inherited all my good points from Dr. Braverman," Bravo said, neutral and expository.

"The voice of Aida Braverman is heard in the land," Glover said. She swung Bravo around and jounced him on her knees. " 'Last night it was, ah, yesternight, between her lips and mine—' Did I ever tell you about my very first audience with tight-assed Aida Braverman? Your progenitor, complete with good points, was called away on a mis-

---

sion of mercy. So there I sat, watching my belly swell and gumming my quid. And in sways Aida. I forget what she is wearing. Either floor-length salmon satin or Sweet Ore overalls. 'I believe,' says Aida, peeping from behind her fan, 'you are acquainted with Dr. David Braverman?' 'Yup,' I says, swatting my womb. 'You are,' says Aida, with pauses for effect, 'looking . . . at . . . his . . . mother.' I hurled myself to the Aubusson, prostrate, dazzled. I rapped my forehead on the Aubusson—once—twice—thrice. 'Boo,' goes Aida Braverman. 'Hoo,' goes Aida Braverman. 'A boo and a hoo and a boo hoo hoo. To think,' says Aida Braverman, 'that *he* should think so little of his mother's only son.' "

"Plenty of people can't tie bows," Bravo said testily.

"Can you read and write? Add and subtract? Divide and multiply?"

"I can lift things up with my toes and I can whistle and tell what cats are thinking and make people cross the street just by looking at them out the window."

"All those accomplishments foretell a rich and various future, Bunnynose, but let me tell you, a man who can't tie his own shoelaces is ultimately going nowhere in this culture."

"I'm not a man," said Bravo, with irritable piety. "I'm just a little child."

"Then get off my lap," Glover said. "Because I never did like little children."

"No," Bravo said, finding handholds.

The telephone began to ring.

"The telephone is ringing," Glover said.

Mysteriously, Bravo increased in weight. "No," he said.

"You shouldn't have flushed my lashes down the toilet last night," Glover said. "That, I hope you realize, was a dishonorable act. And also mean, vicious, and petty. I really wanted to go to that party."

"So you should have went," Bravo said merrily. "With one baldy eye and one with hairs pasted on it."

Glover tried to rise and scrape him off her, but he clung. "I'm going to answer that phone," Glover said.

"No," Bravo said. "It's only Keith."

"Don't you dare talk that way about Keith," Glover said.

"What way?" Bravo said, stalling.

"Use your wits, will you," Glover said. "He's been calling all morning. If nobody answers, he's bound to decide I've murdered you and put my head in the oven."

"If you don't answer the telephone, I might eat a nice soft-boiled egg," Bravo said. His eyes were demurely cast down.

"You haven't eaten a nice soft-boiled egg since the day you were born."

"With toast," Bravo said. "Possibly."

"I want a definite promise," Glover said. "No contingencies."

The telephone stopped ringing. They studied it. "Okay," Glover said. "That tears it. He's on his way over to comb through the wreckage. I hope you're satisfied."

"You're the one who's supposed to *like* him," Bravo said.

"I like him," Glover said, with her arms around Bravo. "I like him, I love him, I adore him, I'm crazy about him. I just happened to be taking *your* feelings into consideration, which is more, I might say, than you ever do mine."

At once the phone began again to ring.

"I'll get it," Bravo said sweetly. "If you'll promise I can come back to the island."

"I'd really better get it myself," Glover said. But Bravo

89

was already at the phone. "Dr. Braverman's residence," he bellowed into the mouthpiece as, almost simultaneously, he flung the instrument into its cradle. He stood with his back to Glover, looking at the silent telephone. She pushed her chair up to her drawing board and began, with industry, to white out a tiny error.

"You said I could come back to the island," Bravo said, without approaching her.

"Did I say that?"

"Not exactly," Bravo said.

"Is this now, or has it ever been, Dr. Braverman's residence?"

"Not exactly," Bravo said.

"I hope it was only Keith," Glover said. "Because however your grandmother Braverman answers the phone in *her* home, this is *my* home, and in *my* home we do not answer the phone by saying this is Dr. Braverman's residence, because it's not. Is that clear?"

"No," Bravo said. "If you drip on your drawing, you'll ruin it."

"I'm not so far gone in the tremblies that I drip on my drawings," Glover said. "Yet." She blew her nose noisily. Aida Braverman was, like herself, a silent sobber and a noisy nose-blower. Probably it was a tribal bond. Possibly she and Aida were in constant, mystic, honking communion.

"She must really be getting her jollies these days," Glover said. "Weekend custody of son and grandson. She must be creaking her stays."

Bravo sat down on the floor with his back to her.

"Was he there?" Glover said carefully.

Bravo began to rock.

"Don't do that," Glover said. "That's all I need."

———

Bravo stopped rocking.

"Was he there or wasn't he there? I'll give you a brand-new green Pentel if you'll answer that simple question."

"You're not supposed to say bad things about him," Bravo said. "And he's not supposed to say bad things about you. It's all in *The Child's Book of Divorce* and Grandmother Braverman is reading me it."

"How is Grandmother Braverman fixed for *The Child's Book of Fire, Famine, Plague, and Pestilence? The Child's Book of Dread? The Child's Book of Despair?* That's an oldie but goodie."

"She has that one," Bravo said. Almost imperceptibly, he began to rock.

"She has *what* one? Stop that!"

"Death," Bravo said. "Would you like a bacon and mashed banana sandwich?"

"No. Would you like a bacon and mashed banana sandwich?"

"No."

"If I make myself a bacon and mashed banana sandwich, will you eat at least two bites of it?"

"Maybe," Bravo said. "If you die, who'll take care of McGonigle and Babycat?"

Glover drank off the sticky remains of her sherry. "Do be sure to mention to your estimable Granny that Mummy has succumbed to booze."

"That's not booze. That's what you pour in the stew."

"Must you refer to everything I cook as 'the stew'?"

"The only reason you drank that is so you can tell Keith you drank it," Bravo said wisely.

"Bravo," Glover said, "look at me." He turned his head and regarded her. "You're a very intelligent child," Glover said. He turned his head away. "I know you asked me a question and I didn't answer it," she said. "Maybe if you ask me again, I'll answer it this time."

Bravo said nothing for a little time and then he said: "What's an albatross?"

"An albatross is a beautiful bird," Glover said. "Like a bird of paradise—with diamonds in its tail. You ate one once. Hand me my sticks and I'll mash you a banana."

Bravo ran into the bedroom and brought back a dandy's walking stick with a fancifully carved handle.

"No," she said, and inclined her head. The aluminum canes she sometimes used were well within her reach, but Bravo, though he hated them, stepped onto the island and gave them to her.

"They're no more disgusting than Aida Braverman's false teeth," Glover said, with a mixture of consolation and malice.

Bravo made a gagging noise.

"Well, I'm sorry," Glover said. "If we lived in a somewhat more sylvan setting, you could wander in the woods and cut mamá a forkéd branch and fashion her a crutch."

"Oh, please," Bravo said.

"Tell me about David," Glover said, moving, with considerable skill, through cats, to the kitchen.

"Tell me about the paradise bird."

"I'll tell if you tell," Glover said. "You go first." She rooted around in the refrigerator for the bacon. The refrigerator was stocked with forlorn and classy rejects, like tinted quail eggs.

"Dr. Braverman is the top man in his field," said Bravo dutifully.

"Not bloody lately," Glover said. "Dr. Braverman is

bonkers. Dr. Braverman is bin-worthy. He went from a nice, clean, obsessive-compulsive, top-man-in-his-field-type chap to a flaky cat who uses his wrists to strop his razor. Did you talk to him?" She arranged the strips of bacon very neatly on the grill.

"No," Bravo said.

"Did he talk to you?"

"A little bit."

"About me?"

"About inner space," Bravo said, and solemnly picked up a cat and solemnly hugged and kissed it.

"He's done for," Glover said, gloomily mashing a banana from a vast banana inventory.

"Did you ever climb in bed with him early in the morning?" Bravo said.

"I believe I may have done that very thing."

"He's nice then," Bravo said. "Sleepy."

"Yes," Glover said, and burned her hand on the grill. "Yes," she said, holding it beneath the tap. "If you catch him just before sunrise, as the dead are returning to their tombs, he is very passable company, as I recall."

"He gave me a sock."

"He *hit* you?"

"A sock, a *sock!*" Bravo yelled. He pulled from his pocket a careful roll of fabric, which, finger-pressed, turned out to be a man's sock with a hole in it.

"Is he dispensing relics?" Glover said, alarmed.

Bravo rolled up the sock and tucked it tidily away.

"I told him could I have it and he said sure I could."

"Oh, my paws and whiskers," Glover said. "I believe you love that son of a bitch."

Although the bacon wasn't ready, she began to assemble

the sandwiches. She was very deft and showy.

"Well, he's a psychologically disturbed person," Bravo said. "We must remember that."

"Ah, me," said Glover, running more water on her damaged fingers. "Me oh my. There are so many things we must remember."

Keith's key was heard in the lock and they started apart like lovers. Keith, all hooded lambskin coat and pink silky hair and heartiness and qualms, came heavily into the kitchen. He was carrying three brown paper bags full of groceries.

"My God," he said at the sight of the canes, "are you bad again? Do you need those?"

"Certainly not," Glover said snappily, though she was glad to see him. "They're just a temporary expedient. Till my plywood platform with the roller skate wheels is delivered from Hammacher Schlemmer."

Bravo laughed immoderately, pounding his knees with his fists.

Keith, a social worker, loved children as a concept, but could never think of anything useful to say to them. He looked helplessly to Glover.

"Quit that," Glover said to Bravo, who quit it.

"He should be in school," Keith said to Glover.

"He was too upset after last night."

"*I* wasn't upset," said Bravo. "*You* were upset."

"I wasn't upset," Glover said.

"*I* was upset," Keith said, in a loud, definitive way.

"*You* didn't flush her lashes down the toilet," Bravo shouted. "*I* did."

"I shouldn't have made such a row," Keith said.

"A row more or less around here is hardly to be noticed," Glover said. "Have a truly repellent sandwich." She took a bite from a sandwich herself and handed it on to Bravo. "Here, Mithradates." Bravo took a bite and handed it back.

"They have peculiar tastes in food, don't they," Keith said, sure that the natives had no knowledge of English.

The sandwich in transit from Glover to Bravo suffered a significant rebuff.

"Thank you very much indeed for dropping in," Glover said.

"My favorite food is paradise bird," Bravo snobbishly told Keith.

"Oh, Christ," Keith said. "Is that what this is?" He took a big bite of mashed banana and underdone bacon and chewed it gallantly.

"*He* isn't very gifted," Bravo told Glover.

"He's one hell of a good sport," Glover said.

"That's the best bird of paradise I ever tasted," Keith said.

"Oh, please," Bravo said. He went to the knife drawer and took out all the knives. Then he plugged in the knife sharpener and proceeded to sharpen or destroy them.

"Is he allowed to do that?" Keith asked in the din.

"Let's put it this way, he isn't *not* allowed to do it."

"Are you all right?" Keith said.

"Splendid. I'm turning slowly into a turnip. My child is half starved and smells like a musk-ox and they're trying to take him away from me. I drove my ex-husband mad and my present lover is planning to abandon me as soon as he finishes putting away the frozen peas. I'm fine."

Keith, meticulously stowing snow peas in the freezer, said, "You didn't drive David mad."

"Oh, sure I did. With two words. Cure me."

———

"David," Keith said, "was known around the hospital as grandiose."

"David," she said, "was known around the *house* as grandiose. Nevertheless, I booted him over the edge."

"You've had a lot of remissions," Keith said chidingly.

"To which of his treatments do I owe those remissions? Protein injections? Zone therapy? Bran baths? Megavitamins? Hypnotism? est? CR? TM? Simple faith? Loving kindness? Vicious abuse?"

"I don't know that," said Keith, busily wrapping and labeling meat. "I just know you're beating the odds."

"I think you're disappointed. You want me to get sick enough so they can get Bravo away from me. But not too sick for *you* to take care of."

"Stop punishing me," Keith said. "I told you the truth last night. I said adultery was a lark compared to this arrangement. And I meant it. Let him stay with Aida for a month or two. She's a perfectly nice, limited, decent woman. She loves him. Let's have a little something of our own. We don't know how long we've got."

"You know, you have a certain mortuary presence," Glover said.

Abruptly, Bravo gave up on the knives.

"Tell about that bird," he shouted, "unless you're lying again."

"He really is an intolerable brat," Keith said without heat. "Even making allowances." He hoisted Bravo up on the counter.

"It isn't so much of a story," Glover said. "When you were a baby, I had long, long hair. And David gave me an antique comb with a bird of paradise on it in brilliants.

96

And you liked it so much, I let you play with it. And you pried out some of the stones and swallowed them. At least I think you did, I never found them. I was terrified. I kept baptizing you and inspecting your diapers. You may to this day have a rhinestone festering in your gut."

"A diamond," Bravo said, complacently patting his belly.

"Didn't you tell David?" Keith said.

"God, no. He'd have had the top man in the field of infant entrails eviscerating my only child."

"You should have told Dr. Braverman," Bravo said. "He's very smart."

"He does give that impression," Glover said. "The first time I saw David, I was sure I was dying. And I was. He took one look at me and jotted something down on my chart. The absolute certainty of it! When he left the room, I grabbed it and it said: 'Slim young woman in no distress.' It's just a medical cliché, but I didn't know that then. Oh, God, I thought. Thank God. Slim young woman in no distress. That's exactly what I want to be. And so I married him."

"It was a little more complex than that," Keith said.

"A little," Glover said, "but not a lot. It got complicated later."

"I wonder why you have a key to my house, but I don't have a key to yours," Bravo said to Keith.

"It's a little bit hard to explain," Keith said.

"That's all right," Bravo said. "I'll just ask Grandmother Braverman."

"Don't," Glover said.

"Yes," Bravo said ominously. "I know what you do when I'm not here."

———

"You know everything," Glover said. "You're the agent of a foreign power."

"If you like my mother so much," Bravo said, "why don't you get married with her?"

"That's Aida Braverman talking," Glover said, "that limited, decent soul."

"Why *don't* you?" Bravo said to Keith.

"Well, tell the child," Glover said. "Go ahead, why *don't* you?"

"Do you really expect me to marry you?" Keith said.

"I think you might try for another reading on that," Glover said.

"If I asked you to marry me, you'd refuse," he said.

"Ask me," she said. "I demand that you ask me."

He put on his coat and pulled the hood up over his head.

"If you need me," he said miserably, "you know how to find me."

•   •   •

That night Glover lay on the couch and Bravo sat astride her. He had let her wash his hands, face, and feet and dry-shampoo his hair.

They were watching McGonigle sink her teeth in the shimmering nape of Babycat. McGonigle braced herself, got a purchase, and heaved. Babycat was, in this way, and to no detectable intent, frequently shifted a very few inches. Babycat, ex-kitten, now the size of a rabbit, submitted stoically to this regime, though his nape and parts, in fact, of his toes had been worn away by it. Glover took a rubber band from around her wrist, made a paper wad from the

Times, and plunked McGonigle in the flank. McGonigle snubbed her.

"That cat is a psychologically disturbed person," Glover said.

Bravo patted her face. "Who all do you love?" he said. He had a good-boy look and he was being winning.

"You," she said obligingly. "My clean and handsome son. Who do you love?"

"Grandmother Braverman," he said. "She lets me hitch her garters."

"That is a particularly foul lie," Glover said, honestly outraged.

"I started with the back ones, which a stout person can't quite reach. And I got so good at those, I moved around to the side ones, and now I do all the front ones, too."

"Get off of me," Glover said. "I promised to call Keith."

"No."

"Get off or I'll dump you off," she said. "I'm calling Keith."

"No!" he said. He raised his fist and smashed it down with all his force. He struck her on the mouth and nose. Her body pitched in pain and he fell and knocked his head against the low glass table. He stared at her, silent, tears streaming. Trickles of dark blood coursed slowly from his nose. She tasted blood in her own mouth and tears of her own were choking her.

"I'm going to call him," she said, not moving.

Bravo pulled himself up on the couch and she opened her arms to receive him. But he ducked beneath her sweater and forced his head up through the neck opening beside hers. He lay upon her bare breasts and his hands

---

probed at her flesh. The ribbing at the neck of the sweater bound them like a noose; their cheeks were made adhesive by tears and blood and snot.

"I *have* to call him," she said in a moment.

"No," he said. "Not right now."

"Not right now," she said, holding his comfortless, bony, small body.

"Not right now."

"Oh, Bravo," she said. "Tell me. How did I get to where I am from where I was?"

"Not now," said Bravo. "Not right now."

———

Old Hag,
You Have
Killed Me

"It wasn't me stuck that ham knife in your father," Minnie
Riley says. Frail and fractious, improbably pretty and im-
possibly old, she has still the husky young carrying voice of
a beleaguered Irish beauty.

"Keep her volume down," Minnie's son, Gerald, says to
his twin, Mary Kate.

"I don't see any knob on her to control the volume, actually," his other, younger, sister, Clare, says.

"Tell her to put a sock in it," Gerald says. "I'm sincere
about this."

"He's sincere," Clare says to Mary Kate.

"He's always sincere," Mary Kate says.

"Jesus," Gerald says. "This is a hospital, this is the middle of the night. Our father may be seriously ill."

"Our father is dead as a mackerel," Clare says.

"You know Gerald," says Mary Kate, "given to understatement."

"Looking on the brighter side," says Clare.

"I'm after telling you that it wasn't me put the ham knife in your father," Minnie says. "Why are you none of you listening to me?"

"Tell her to belt up," Gerald says.

"Don't talk to her like that, Gerry; she's your mother."

"I'm quite aware she's my mother, you ninny," Gerald says, "and I'm not talking to her like that, I'm talking to you like that."

"I say," says Minnie Riley, "and I see I'm obliged to say it again: It wasn't me stuck your father. I couldn't stick a pig."

"No more she could," says Mrs. Cusack. "Couldn't clean a chicken if her life depended on it. Hasn't the stomach for it. Never had. You see me now, I've wrung many an old hen's neck and never felt the worse for it after."

"Jesus Christ," Gerald says. "Everything happens to me. Where is this fool of a woman's fool of a son? Get him to get her out of here."

"I take no offense," says Mrs. Cusack, "for I'm sure none is intended. But I'm not deaf, you know. That's your mammy who's a little dull of hearing; my hearing is the hearing of a girl, says the doctor. He says: 'Mrs. Cusack, you've the hearing of a girl.' It's because I had my ears pierced very young."

"Oh, that's fascinating," Clare says. "Do go on."

"Where is Bunny Cusack?" Gerald demands. "If somebody tells me Bunny Cusack is delivering a baby at a moment like this, I personally will feed him a knuckle sandwich."

"It was a cork held behind the lobe," Mrs. Cusack says, "a darning needle, a great big poker of a thing, heated in the fire, open fires as we had them days, this of course was at home, across the water, as Big Bob used to say. Thrust it through, my sister did, whilst my mother was out on a message. Left a nasty little dangle of black thread. I had to pull on it every day so as to keep the hole open."

"I've often wanted to open a hole in you, Mrs. Cusack," Clare says pleasantly.

"Speaking of threads, I've lost one," Mary Kate says. "I thought the Ma and the big C were on the outs."

Mrs. Cusack, Minnie's friend, neighbor, confidante, and enemy, a hunched old woman who uses a wheeled walker to get about, is as lively as Minnie, though not so pretty and not so deaf. Sometimes she and Minnie have a falling out; once they had no commerce for years, but they've known each other since they were young and tonight they are holding hands.

"I'm sorry for your trouble, Mrs. Riley, dear," Mrs. Cusack hoots in Minnie's ear.

"No, you're not," Clare says. "Let go of her. You're just an old bundle of malice and hair nets and mischief and Ace bandages and you ruined my life once and you're not going to do it again. The death of her father is a watershed experience in a woman's life and I won't have you ruining it for me."

"Has she drink taken?" Mrs. Cusack asks Gerald.

"Why did you call Bunny Cusack when this happened, instead of calling me?" Gerald shouts at his mother.

"Gerry, you destroyed yourself entirely when you saw fit

to destroy your hair," his mother replies, "and that shoe polish fools nobody."

Gerald has had hair transplants. Hair that once grew on the back of his head is well to the front of it now. It has taken on a life of its own, fountaining out like the fronds of a palm tree. Undependable in color as well, it's been touched up a bit. A barber's towel has cleared two crescents in the dye above his ears in an attempt to give him distinguished temples.

"Is she in shock?" Gerald says to Mary Kate. "Is she claiming she called Bunny Cusack instead of me because she prefers the way he combs his hair?"

"He has no hair," Mary Kate says.

"He had good hair when we were young," Clare says. "Bright red hair like Daddy's."

"Bunny never had red hair," Gerald says, dismissingly. "Bunny was called Bunny because he resembled an albino when he was born. Or a newt. Or a bunny."

"Bunny is a doctor," Minnie Riley says, "and the old man was bleeding."

"And Bunny is eldest," Mrs. Cusack says.

"A sort of doctor," Gerald says.

"An obstetrician is not just a sort of doctor," Clare says, "he's a doctor."

"Robert Cusack is an excellent doctor," Minnie says.

"And eldest," Mrs. Cusack says.

"You didn't use him when you gave birth, I made note of that," Gerald says to Clare.

"How could I do that? We had a history," Clare says. "Really, Gerry, you're disgusting."

"Mar used him; later my girls used him. My second wife

———

said he had breath like an otter, but she used him. Barb will probably use him, although I personally don't see much in him, myself."

"In your dreams," Mary Kate says. "That's where Barbara will need an obstetrician." Mary Kate puts her hand on Minnie's knee and leans in close. "Imagine him starting another family at his age?" she shouts at Minnie, scandalized.

"Who's this?" Minnie says.

"Gerry and his little Barb person are planning on having *babies*," Mary Kate shouts.

"Sure, what do I care who has babies?" Minnie says mildly.

"Leave them to it," Mrs. Cusack says. "Let them have a go at it. Live and let live, that's my motto and my credo."

"In your hat," Clare says. "Excuse me, but."

"Bunny is talking to the police," Minnie says.

"Polis," Clare says. "Don't you love the way she says that? She says 'organization,' too, with the long *i*, like in the IRA on television. She's so cute." She hugs her mother's shoulders and kisses her flossy crown.

"She says Eye-talian, too," Mary Kate says. "That was cute when I was married to Guido. Guido thought it was so cute, she nearly wound up with her feet in cement."

"Did you make a statement?" Gerald says. "To the authorities?"

"A what?" Minnie says. "Don't slouch like that, Gerry, and do not mumble."

"What did you tell the police?"

"Nothing, nothing. I had no conversation with them beyond 'hello how are you.' "

" 'Hello how are you' and the old man's bleeding like—

105

bleeding? Is this possible? Surely you told them something?"

"No, nothing. Not at all."

"Good," Gerald shouts, and shows her a thumbs-up.

"Throw your shoulders back, Gerry, and don't be quacking in my face like a duck."

"Odd, though. You're sure you said nothing?"

"Nothing, only the truth."

"Jesus, I knew it," Gerald says. "The truth."

"Could this be really calamitous?" Clare says. "I mean, it's not like murder one, or whatever; there are extenuating circumstances, surely. Not that I know what they are, but he was a dreadful old man and he surely had it coming. In her place I'd have done it long ago."

"Shut up, you adulterous little slut, or I'll throw you out of here. Why does everything happen to me?"

"Because you're destiny's plaything," Mary Kate says. "And don't you talk to Clare like that. She's upset and she's your sister."

"You're not serious, I thought she was Oprah Winfrey."

"Is he dead yet?" Minnie Riley says.

"As a mackerel," Clare says. "I don't know if I'm upset or I'm not upset."

"Keep us informed," Mary Kate says, swabbing purple slime off her neck and forehead as she has been for an hour, using up her roll of paper towels.

"A murder rap," Clare says, "the big house, the chair. I'm trying to see how I feel about things. Two old people like they are, who'd believe a thing like that."

"The four of us for starters," Mary Kate says.

"Big Bob has come through worse and been the better for it," Mrs. Cusack says. "I mind the time he fell off the ladder and didn't they arrest him for Peeping Tom."

———

Gerald says, "Of course this incident was an accident, but I believe we may need a lawyer."

"Gerry, you are a lawyer."

"I'm not that kind of lawyer, as you know."

"You're a crooked lawyer is what I know," Clare says.

"All right, all right, I'm sorry I said what I said."

"I'm not an adulterous slut," Clare says.

"Only because she's got too old for it," Mrs. Cusack says. "Got past it."

"Well, I'm not a crooked lawyer, either," Gerald says.

"Mary Kate, what is all over your head? Wash that material out of your head. This is not the time nor place to be showing yourself in that condition."

"Ma, really," Mary Kate says, swabbing. "I was coloring my hair when I got the call and it just felt wrong to wash all the slop off before I rushed to the hospital to see my dying father. If he is dying. It seemed like vanity, as if I loved my good appearance more than I loved my father."

"Do you love your father, Mary Kate?" asks Minnie. "It's a wonder if you do because he gave you an awful life as a child if you want my honest opinion."

"He used to say, 'It isn't shoes Mary Kate needs for feet the size of hers. It's the boxes they come in,' " Clare says helpfully.

"Oh, did he really? That slipped my mind. If I'd remembered that, of course it'd make all the difference. The things he did and said to me and that's all you remember? You really are out to lunch."

"He is crooked, Gerald," Mrs. Cusack says to Minnie. "That townhouse complex he developed, he filled that mucky ground with bits of trash and now it's all swales and sinkholes, wee houses tumbling in, sure they fear for their

---

lives there. My niece, a tree before her house, it was sucked under, sucked under and her looking at it, could as well have been a child."

"Mrs. Cusack, she can't hear you," Clare says.

"Nonsense, hears perfect. She's wearing her device."

"God," Gerald groans. "Some one of you find out what she said to the cops."

"What's with you? Can't talk to her yourself? Your permit's lapsed?" Clare says.

"Big Bob may come round, you know," Minnie Riley says. "He may fare well, be quite all right. Right as rain."

"God forfend," Mary Kate says.

"Do you mind the time he went unhinged for ladies' undergarments?" Mrs. Cusack says to Minnie.

"Pinched them off the clothes reels in the yards," Mrs. Cusack says. "Not many electrical dryers in the olden time." Mrs. Cusack and Minnie hold on to each other, laughing silently.

"Never," Mary Kate says. "Never happened."

"A great man he was for the letters," Minnie says. "A passion he had for the poison pen."

"And the anonymous phone call; he'd take years off your life with one," Mrs. Cusack says.

"Nasty ideas and dirty habits," Minnie says.

"A reprobate," Mrs. Cusack says, "a rotter and a rounder. Not a nice sort of person at all."

"But entertaining in its way," Minnie says, "once you knew he'd never lift a hand to you. And a good provider. I'll feel the loss of it."

"I've had my fill of it," Mrs. Cusack says. "He raised his hand to me often enough."

"Well, sure, you were the love match."

———

"What about it? Didn't you meet him yourself at a cross-roads dance?"

"I did. But then he settled on you and that was all about that," Minnie says.

"A handsome man in his younger days. A bull of a man, much like Bunny."

"Do you mind the time after Bunny was born, a wee babby Bunny was and Big Bob had him in his arms, red-heads, the pair of them, and the bus driver said to Bob, 'You'll not deny that one, mate.' I didn't know where to look, my face was flaming. There I was, far gone with the twins, and there you were with Bunny."

"Bunny was the spit of him."

"The three of us," Minnie says comfortably, laughing.

"The six of us," Mrs. Cusack says in a naughty way. "Two of us as yet unborn." The old women laugh together.

"Sure where was Cusack, was he dead yet?"

"Oh, he was, of course he was, months before that. I wouldn't do a thing to shame Cusack, though I hated Cusack," Mrs. Cusack says.

"Spiteful old devil he was. I mind the time you crept off to the Rockaways."

"With my sister, Tillie Lafferty, as she then was."

"With Big Bob."

"Well."

"Sick? Puking your guts up. Pregnant."

"Didn't know it. Terrified as well."

"What did you find when you returned?"

"Cusack hadn't flushed the toilet in the two weeks I was gone."

"Not a nice sort of man, that."

"No fun in him."

———

109

"Big Bob hated him," Minnie says.

"Big Bob had his reasons," Mrs. Cusack says merrily.

"What in God's name could Bunny Cusack be saying to the cops all this time?" Gerald says. "I thought he had pull here, I thought he was capable of handling this situation."

"Step in, why don't you?" says his sister Mary Kate.

"These old chicks are committable," Clare says, "but they'll never serve a day."

"Do you mind the time Big Bob threw the caustic out the attic window to blight poor Cusack's garden?" Mrs. Cusack says, rocking. "And the wind took the spray and blew it back down the side of your house. The evidence, all black and horrible, there for all to see."

"And Big Bob had to get the house faced in brick. Served him right."

"Big Bob hated Cusack," Mrs. Cusack says contentedly.

"Do you think Bob poisoned him?"

"Jesus Christ," Gerald says. "Please, God, send Bunny Cusack in to save me."

"Sometimes I think Bob did, sometimes I think he did not. Cusack, dead of a mushroom."

"I've thought on that many's the time," Minnie says with genuine pleasure. "What ever made Cusack think Big Bob knew a wild mushroom from a pot cloth? Big Bob wasn't from country places, he was a city man."

"Sure when Bob was a lad on the other side, even the city places was country places. To do him justice. There are books, you know. Pictures of the mushrooms, various kinds and designations."

"Mrs. Cusack, Bunny was my first lover," Clare says. "Bunny had me in the front seat of a green Studebaker. He knew so little about it, he kicked the car in gear and we shot out into traffic."

"Did you ever hear the like?"

"Pay her no mind; our Clare itches where she daren't scratch."

"Did Mrs. Cusack say 'hello how are you' to the cops by any chance?" says Gerald with deep dread.

"I had a word with them. I did."

"The father was a torture to these children so he was; I blame them for nothing," Minnie says. "Or not much."

"Yes, but had I married Bunny Cusack, my whole life would have taken on a new dimension," Clare says. "And you broke it up."

"Is she daft?" Minnie says to Gerald. "At a time like this, no thought for others."

"Did you ever see a turnip carved into a jack-o'-lantern on the other side, Minnie Riley?" Mrs. Cusack says. "For Halloween or anything else?"

"Maybe in country places."

"There's books, pictures of such as that," Mrs. Cusack says.

"How's that for cute, 'boooks,' she pronounces it, with three or four o's. How's that for cute?" Mary Kate says to Clare.

"The thing about Big Bob, should you caution him not to do a thing, that is the very thing he does be doing," Minnie says.

"Tell him the only thing you can carve with a ham knife is a ham. He does what his own divil bids him and this is his comeuppance," Mrs. Cusack says.

"Och, aye," Minnie says. "He was carving the turnip for

———

you, Mrs. Cusack. He thought that would get my goat."

"So it would," Mrs. Cusack says, laughing.

"So it would," Minnie says, joining in. "The state of my kitchen. Stabbed himself in the groin of the leg. A wee slit of a wound, but you couldn't stanch it."

"No," Mrs. Cusack says. "Did you put him into his good suit yourself? I ask because I put the new pajamas on Cusack and I hope to God never again to dress a dead man, they're that unwieldy."

"Aye," Minnie says, "I wish I had time to tidy that kitchen, but Bunny said not."

"No, Mrs., Bunny knows."

"They say if you put a mushroom to a silver spoon, the spoon will turn black if it's poison."

"So they say, but it's not so; don't trust it."

"I won't, then."

"Did the wee slits line up, Mrs. Riley?" Mrs. Cusack murmurs. "There was a wee slit in the trousers, no doubt."

"They was very good trousers," Minnie Riley says, "though sodden with blood. Lovely material."

"If the wee slits don't line up, our Bunny will see to it and we'll say no more about it," Mrs. Cusack says.

"I think the world of Bunny Cusack," Minnie Riley says. "We all do, all belonging to me."

"God help me," Gerald says.

And then Dr. Cusack bounds into the room. All surgical greens, clean hands, and capable expression. Wicked. And radiant, with the cast-off light of his dead father.

Robbed

Janet D'Arcy is fumbling through a display in the back of Mrs. Riordan's jewelry store, in search of a certain kind of wedding ring, when the thief, up front, shows Mrs. Riordan his gun.

"Jesus, Mary, and Joseph," Mrs. Riordan says in a clear, childlike tone, so affronted, so reverent, and so startling that it lifts the hairs on Janet's neck.

Janet considers calling out, "Is everything okay?" in a cheerful way, just as filler, but she knows at once that Mrs. Riordan has had a vision or a stroke. Queasily, guiltily, she yearns to scoop up handfuls of wedding rings, months' supply, and tiptoe, past enlightenment, past catastrophe, out the door and back into her own dilemmas.

Instead she says, "I'm coming, I'm coming," as though it were she who has been summoned, and walks into the front room of the shop. Mrs. Riordan is taking jewelry from a drawer and dropping it into a canvas camera bag. Her touch looks deft and indifferent, as though she were trafficking in potatoes or lumps of coal; it lacks the finicky, pious deference she usually accords her commonplace stock.

"That's it for the layaway," Mrs. Riordan says to the man who stands at the counter. "See?" She has pulled out the drawer and holds it upside down to prove that it is empty.

"That's perfectly okay, miss," the man says. "That's totally okay, I take your word for it. Now the diamonds, then the watches, high end only." The man is unexceptional-looking for this rather elegant small town; he wears the kind of clothes Janet's husband wears around town, navy blue watch cap, good parka, corduroys.

"Excuse me," Janet says, like a fool.

It is then that she sees the gun, repugnant, small and silver-colored, held very still at about the level of his crotch. It is pointing at Mrs. Riordan, but when he sees Janet, the man shifts his weight and now the gun is pointing at Janet.

"That's not a real gun," Janet says, although she is convinced and enraged by the gun and wants to leap upon the man and pummel him for pointing a gun at her. "That's not a real gun," Janet says. "I saw one like it in the Best catalog. It's an air gun, it just shoots beebees or bolts. Fifteen ninety-five." She is trembling with fury and with fear.

"*Bolts,*" Mrs. Riordan says, appalled. "My word."

"Who invited you to this party?" the man says to Janet.

Robbed

He is calm and mild. "This lady and I, we wanted to be alone."

"Oh, for God's sake, that woman's never out of here," Mrs. Riordan says. "She hangs around and hangs around until I could scream."

"You astonish me," Janet says. "I know this is very stressful, but the point is not to insult a good customer, the point is to stand up to this man. He is trying to steal from you, he is taking what belongs to you; don't collaborate in that."

"Dry up," Mrs. Riordan says. She has unlocked a glass case and now sweeps engagement rings impatiently into piles and flings the piles into the canvas bag.

"Those are diamond rings," Janet says. "Those are not salted peanuts."

"Could you gag her, maybe, something like that?" Mrs. Riordan says to the gunman. "She shreds my nerves."

"Lie down," the gunman says to Janet, who can no longer see him, who sees instead an IdentiKit face, crudely drawn in heavy lines, a store brand male face: two eyes, eyebrows, nose, mustache, nothing extra, nothing special, nothing fancy, pure ferocity. "Lie down, I told you," the gunman says politely, "please, miss."

"Never," Janet says, but she is kneeling. The gunman tells her to get behind the counter and she knee-walks back there, stretches out. "All my instincts tell me you're not the kind of person who does this," Janet says. "Only God knows what kind of tragedy in life has brought you to this pass."

Mrs. Riordan, on her way to the watches, treads on Janet's hand.

———

115

"Don't take her watch, take my watch," Mrs. Riordan says, peeling her watch off. "She's an eccentric person. She has 'Daniel and Janet forever' on the back of that watch, I guarantee you. 'Daniel and Janet forever' gives me the jumps."

"Daniel is my husband. I don't find that eccentric. Why is that eccentric, Mrs. Riordan?"

"I have engraved 'Daniel and Janet forever' on the insides of maybe ten or twelve wedding rings for this one," Mrs. Riordan says, not to Janet.

"Mine is a Cartier tank watch," Janet says, as Mrs. Riordan binds her hands and ankles under the gunman's direction. "You people don't know your own trades."

"Don't hurt us," Mrs. Riordan breathes as she in turn is trussed. "Don't hurt us."

"You don't know where I'm coming from, where I'm going, where I'm at," gently says the gunman, but Mrs. Riordan whimpers as his bonds bite her flesh.

When he has gone, the women lie there, estranged and intimate and peaceful. Janet studies Mrs. Riordan's pretty, piggy feet in strappy shoes. "I never even knew you didn't like me," Janet says, sweet-voiced and wooing.

Mrs. Riordan bucks her bundled feet.

"Where's the button?" Janet says. "The alarm switch? The thing that rings in the police station?"

"You see too many movies."

"Oh, but surely."

"Ask me about the insurance," Mrs. Riordan says. "I figure I'm roughly thirty thousand ahead. Roughly. Because I don't have insurance. But if I did, it would set me back maybe sixty thousand. So not having any, if he took thirty thousand, which he easily did, that's thirty thousand ahead. More or less, without pencil and paper."

"Should we scream?" Janet says.

"You scream. I'm resting up my stamina. But scream. Pretend you're at home. Or work loose a few of these knots with your teeth, if you'd rather."

"I don't actually think I could do that," Janet says. "Why did you say I was eccentric? I just lose my wedding ring constantly; I don't find that eccentric. I'm a television producer, I work very hard, I get tired. I'm on location. I can't sleep in my wedding ring, so I take it off and put it in the ashtray on the bedside table in some hotel and we have an early call and I've kissed another wedding ring good-bye. I don't do it on purpose."

"I sleep in a custom-made brassiere and a partial bridge and sometimes my contacts," Mrs. Riordan says to the ceiling and the rug. "But this one can't sleep in her wedding ring."

"I don't deny it's somewhat psychological," Janet says with dignity, addressing Mrs. Riordan's instep. "I have a very difficult marriage."

"If every woman with a difficult marriage let it lap up her attention, let alone her common sense," says Mrs. Riordan, "the world would be a worse mess than it is even."

"You don't know my husband," Janet says.

"I do know your husband, yes, I do. Clean-cut. Soft-spoken. Nice sort of fellow, see him running. Super legs, fuzzy lip, glum expression. Something along the lines of the guy who robbed the store."

"Not at all," Janet says.

"I express an opinion."

"We should scream," Janet says. "Daniel's nothing like the man who robbed the store." But Daniel of "Daniel and

Janet forever" is joined in Janet's mind with the gunman. "I need another wedding ring," says Janet desperately. "I can't go round with my hand in my pocket. I can't go round with a glove. I know a man who bought a gross of wedding rings because he always lost his ring playing squash. He bought a gross, wholesale. Nobody said he was eccentric. Everybody said he was cute."

"I'll get you a gross. Wholesale. Not engraved."

"I'll go mad before I work my way through one hundred and forty-four wedding rings, my God. And they have to be engraved, it's the only way it's honorable. Look, I know this is all idiotic, but that's beside the point."

"When last I had occasion to call the police," says Mrs. Riordan, "it was just because of a big snake in my wood-pile. So the chief drives up in the chief car and he's trembling, he can't get out. Scared of snakes. Wants my sympathy. Chief of police."

"Well, he demonstrated moral courage," Janet says. "Admitting his frailty. You must admire that."

"I don't need some guy with moral courage shaking in my driveway. I need some guy with a shovel, smacking my snake."

"Were you ever in Glee Club? In Choir? I could count off like a downbeat and we could scream in unison, duet. Would that embarrass you? This is your place of business, after all, not mine, but I feel it's going to look not very well if we don't scream."

"Oh, some poor soul will wander by looking for a toilet or a telephone," Mrs. Riordan says. "And that will be that. And you'll never come in my shop again, thank God. No lurking. No buying those hideous estate items. No earrings you'll never wear. No charms shaped like squirrels for a bracelet you never owned. No slipping it in like an onion you forgot, one wedding ring, engraved, what's-'is-name loves what's-'is-name forever."

"You have no heart," says Janet D'Arcy.

"You have no guts," Mrs. Riordan replies.

In due course an elderly man pops in, looking to have a cuff link soldered. He doesn't scream exactly, but he makes a lot of noise and rouses the multitude. Released to a throng, the women sob and tremble, hug and howl and contradict each other. Mrs. Riordan shouts that she is ruined. Janet D'Arcy screams that she has nearly been beaten, nearly raped, nearly murdered, meanly snubbed. Screams that the gunman looks exactly like her husband. Mrs. Riordan shouts no such a thing. Daniel D'Arcy comes, sullen and accusing. His screaming wife leaps onto him and pounds him with her loving fists. Alarmed, he kisses her. Screaming face, flailing, naked, loving fingers. "Daniel D'Arcy," Janet screams. "Daniel, I can't bear it. Daniel, Daniel," Janet D'Arcy screams. "Daniel, *we've been robbed.*"

O Lovely
Appearance
of Death

Regina Monahan, five years old, sat sweaty and frog-legged on the grass matted floor of the porch. Her forehead bulged the tarnished screen. She breathed its foreign, tinny odor and studied through it the disobliging, cross-hatched world. Meridian Street was desolate, shadowless, and hot. Regina's throat ached, her ears hurt, she could barely talk or swallow. Her new Crayolas softened in the sun beside her. Four days earlier she'd had her tonsils out. Today was the third of July.

Up the block, out of sight, a string of Chinese firecrackers burst with a rat-a-tat-tat. Somebody jumping the gun. Regina made a face. Nothing suited her.

Behind the open windows of his office, Regina's uncle Hughie urged a wisdom tooth from the nervous, bleeding jaw of a stout girl named Mrs. McKenzie. Mrs. McKenzie was moaning in a very depressing way. Uncle Hughie kept telling her she couldn't feel a thing. Some one of the devices he had her hooked up to made a gruesome sizzling and sputter. "Theodore," Mrs. McKenzie moaned, as best she could through a mouthful of clamps and pliers. "Oh, Theodore, why don' you he'p me?" Theodore was Mr. McKenzie, but he wasn't anywhere around. He was down on Jericho Turnpike, selling Pontiacs in the sunshine. Mrs. McKenzie was purely on her own. "Now then," Regina's uncle Hughie soothed, in a way that would make you want to bite his hand, "now now then, now, now."

The living room and Uncle Hughie's waiting room and office were on opposite sides of the hall. In the living room Regina's aunt Eileen and Mrs. Martin, who lived across the street, tilted toward each other from the edges of their slipcovered chairs, drinking homemade sarsaparilla and having one of their creepy conversations. Their woe-is-me voices rose and fell—marital discord, female disease, the ways and means to clean wallpaper, Mrs. Crestlake. They called Mrs. Crestlake That One. Mrs. Crestlake was Regina's secret friend, but nobody else liked her at all.

Regina was looking at Mrs. Crestlake's house, and had been looking at it almost constantly since morning. It was the corner house on the other side of the street, two houses down from Mrs. Martin's, bigger and farther back from the sidewalk than any of the other houses and, in Regina's opinion, much more interesting. Mrs. Crestlake's house was the only one on Meridian Street that had had its old screened porch ripped off. Its renovated front looked tender and exposed, although the alteration was a year or more old, and cockeyed—as though an impetuous apprentice without a ruler had taken a guess at how things would turn out and been dismally surprised. Mrs. Crestlake's house was a high-spirited, out-of-scale fiasco, with everything on it. In the middle of the muddle of bay windows, wooden lace, captain's walk, red awnings, blue fieldstone, and so on, was an oversize vaulted white door, gaudy with things nobody else on Meridian Street had so far thought of: a colored glass jigsaw puzzle window, like a church window, Regina thought, but without a holy picture; a brass-bound peephole; a big brass door pull shaped like the hilt of Excalibur; a big brass knocker in the shape of a snarling lion, a painful ring stuck through his nose.

The hedge around the property was not very high, but it reared up into wishing wells and Ali Baba urns. Bushes mobbed the lawn. Clipped and trained with string like the hedge, they'd been turned into poodles jumping through hoops, seals juggling stars, baskets with handles and ribbon bows, just like the dinky fluted paper kind Regina got at birthday parties, filled with sugar chicken corn. The bushes needed tending; their outlines were blurred. Almost hidden among them stood a pink plaster one-legged bird and a silver-green ball on a post.

Regina's aunt Eileen said the place was trashy. She said she couldn't tell was it Coney Island or hell at high noon. Regina thought it was beautiful.

Mrs. Crestlake was beautiful, too, and very interesting. She had pulled out all her eyebrows and drew new ones with a pencil. She went all the way into New York City to have her hair marcelled, and she had never washed it by herself her whole life long—she said that it would make her sick to do that, there was something about hair that was disgusting. In between the times she went to New York City, she squirted her waves with lacquer from a blue bottle and they were as stiff and dull and golden as the wig on Regina's Shirley Temple doll. They were also inflammable. Once she had burned off two or three of the front ones trying to light her Herbert Tarryton cigarette.

When Mrs. Crestlake put on all her bracelets, as she had for Regina, they went right up solid from her wrists to where her muscles were, and she couldn't bend her arms if she wanted to. When Mrs. Crestlake opened her closets and drawers, extraordinary things jumped out at you: things that glittered, things that shone, kimonos made of iridescent changing-color taffeta, yellow satin blouses covered with bugle beads, nightgowns with fur on them, gloves with fringe, a pocketbook with most of a stuffed alligator prone across its flap.

Mrs. Crestlake often said that she was bored skinny, and it was true that she was one of the skinniest people Regina knew. Every stitch of clothes she put on her back had to be taken in miles because her glands were out of whack. Despite this hardship she had thirty-four dresses, a good many of them red or black or red *and* black, and a fancy pair of pants she called her "jod-furs." Nearly every day she put on the pants, flabbergasting most of Meridian Street, and went over to the stables on the other side of town to ride up and down on a big black horse named Turk. On Regina's advice, Mrs. Crestlake fed Turk sugar. Regina knew for a fact that sugar was appropriate to horses as peanuts to elephants or tin cans to goats, but it was news to Mrs. Crestlake.

One of the best things about Mrs. Crestlake was the

things she didn't know. Another good thing about her was the things she did know—or anyway, the things she said, which were, if not useful, informative. She said that if most people weren't so two-faced, they'd admit that children spooked them as much as they did her (she always added, "No offense meant"); she said that when all was said and done men were phoney-baloneys; that it took a lady elephant two years to have a baby; that many, many people had taken her for Myrna Loy. Regina had a standing invitation to drop in on Mrs. Crestlake anytime the spirit moved her. She'd been over there twice that morning, taking a roundabout route through the backyards, but Mrs. Crestlake wasn't home.

•   •   •

"Reggie, Reggie," Aunt Eileen called from the living room, launching her bothered Irish voice on the hot afternoon, "Re-jeen-*a*."

Regina heaved a theatrical sigh and went squinting into the living room, where the women were. The blinds were shut against the sun, but a little spilled in anyway, making gilt stains on the ceiling and on the flowered rug.

"Hello, Lambie," Mrs. Martin said out of the pink gloom, "how do you feel?"

"Fine, thank you," Regina murmured, keeping out of reach, making a horrible face at the floor.

"Does your poor throat hurt you?" Mrs. Martin had the mocking jowl of a camel, misallied with a piteous manner, as of one who persevered in the face of a recent bereavement. She was a cheek-pincher and a chin-chucker and she made Regina nervous.

———

"No, it does not," Aunt Eileen said positively. "Don't be putting ideas in her head."

"Yes, it does," Regina whispered.

"Now, don't be giving me that," Aunt Eileen said, getting very red. "It wasn't me that did it to you. I had my orders from your parents."

"You never," Regina said.

"I did, I tell you," Aunt Eileen said. "They make me sick, the pair of them, a couple of weak sisters. Dennis is worse than Rita and Rita is worse than Dennis again. They put one over on me that time. 'It has to be done this summer,' they tell me. 'Nothing to signify. Snip, snip, the child won't know the difference.' They couldn't do the deed themselves, but I'm taken to have no feelings."

"Phooey on you," Regina said.

"Regina!" said Mrs. Martin.

"I don't blame the child," Aunt Eileen said. "When they wheeled her out of the operating room and let me look at her, I couldn't draw breath. She was white as wax. Pretty as a big French doll and the color of death. Merciful God, I thought, I've killed her! I thought I'd never get over it."

"I wish I died," Regina said spitefully.

"Well, you didn't," said Aunt Eileen, "so sit down and button your lip."

Regina sat down on the Leatherette hassock. It was tacky from the heat. Aunt Eileen and Mrs. Martin wore ankle socks and blunt flat shoes, like the squeaking shoes of the nurses in the hospital. Mrs. Crestlake nearly always wore high heels. Regina's mother wore high heels, but not as high as Mrs. Crestlake's. Nevertheless, Regina believed her mother had the prettiest feet in the world. She was fond of making lists and she began one of the people with the prettiest feet. She put her mother at the top and then Mrs. Crestlake and then herself. After that she lost interest. Regina glared at Mrs. Martin and her aunt Eileen, despising them for their homely feet and their bare white shiny legs. She wished Mrs. Martin would go up in smoke and her mother would be sitting there. But her mother was in Lake George, with her father and her Grandmother Monahan, crankier and happier than Regina had ever known her, and getting more secret and more swollen every minute, from the baby that was growing in her stomach. If it took a lady elephant two years to have a baby, how long did it take a lady lady? Regina had been worried from the start of the thing, and now she was moving toward panic.

". . . close to her time?" Mrs. Martin was wanting to know.

"Oh, a long many weeks yet," Aunt Eileen said uneasily, "a way yet, thank God. She's mad altogether, I don't mind telling you. She suffered the tortures of the damned when a 'certain person' put in her appearance."

Mrs. Martin shot her eyes at Regina and back to Aunt Eileen. "Little pit*chers*," she sang on a rising note, hardly moving her mouth.

"Oh, it's water off a duck's back to her, what does she know? She's had four misses—Rita—and she's damned and determined to carry full term. It's a sin and a shame. It's a mortal crime. She was always delicate."

"Does the husband have a say in it?" Mrs. Martin asked, in such a hopeful, veiled, and ladylike manner that Regina knew she was talking code.

"Dennis Monahan does as he's bid," Aunt Eileen said gloomily. "Lovey-dovey Dennis, if the rain would fall on him, he'd melt. Ten years married and it would make you

blush to look at them, mooning over other like a pair of soppy kids. She was always delicate. 'This one'll carry you off,' I said, 'and you'll leave the child you've already got behind you'—but she's baby this and baby that till there's no peace with her. 'Keep your head,' I said to her, 'it's only a little bit of a fish, it's no baby at all yet.' She says, 'It has an immortal soul, Eileen'—that's my sister Rita. God save us all, but the cat and the divil must have something. 'Don't start in on *that*,' I said. 'It hasn't blue eyes and a bonnet yet, so keep your head.' She's raving mad. It wouldn't be me. If I had the one, that would do me."

"She's a good woman," Mrs. Martin said lugubriously. "She's got love in her heart for the human race. A thing like that brings tears to my eyes."

"Tears, my foot," said Aunt Eileen. "The human race, my foot. She's got love in her heart for Dennis Monahan, and that and a nickel gets a ride on the subway."

"Some women have it easy," Mrs. Martin said, and the tears in her eyes gave way to the light of malice. "Look at That One."

"Isn't it the truth," said Aunt Eileen. "Her that wouldn't turn her toe where her heel would lie has that fine black brute of a husband. And my sister Rita, a saint among women, has Dennis Monahan, the last rose of summer tied up in a clout."

"I don't know that I envy her," Mrs. Martin said. "Painted hussy. Nothing to do but ride her hobbyhorse and get herself up like the dog's breakfast. And as for him, he's not even white meat. He's some kind of a Bulgarian and his name was never Crestlake or I'll eat my hat."

"All the same, she wants for nothing," Aunt Eileen said stubbornly. "She comes and she goes as she pleases; neither chick nor child to worry her and never a by-your-leave. There's plenty to be said for that. It's true enough, he's away a lot, and she's left there to herself."

"I wish *mine* would go away," Mrs. Martin said.

"Don't I wish *mine* would," said Aunt Eileen. "And she has her car and money in her pocket and I suppose she has friends on the order of herself." She plucked a handkerchief opulently bordered in green tatted lace from the sleeve of her housedress and wiped her freckled neck with it. She was, as she said, on the slippery side of forty-five, and handsome in a bold, high-colored way that made her furious. Her hair was a showy, rosy bronze that might have done very well for a dahlia, but seemed a gorgeous mistake on a human head, and a pretty flush rode her cheekbones. She tried to subdue her lovely hair by dousing it with strong black tea, she clandestinely powdered with talcum, but the results did not please her. When her husband told her, as he often did, that she was a fine figure of a woman and as fresh-complected as a bride, she burned red with vexation, shut her eyes and her mouth, made scornful, expiring noises, and advised him, finally, that all that was asked of her at her time of life was neatness, and if he thought it brought her any joy, strive as she would to be neat, to turn out looking, at her time of life, like a baby's well-spanked bottom, he was *wrong*.

Aunt Eileen tucked her handkerchief away and immediately pulled it out again. "I pray God no harm comes to her," she said unhappily. "I've the awfulest feeling that something's in store."

"No harm comes to the likes of That One," Mrs. Martin said.

"Rita, I mean," Aunt Eileen said, and sighed. Regina

sighed, too, and Aunt Eileen looked over at her, repentant and alarmed. "I forgot all about you, Divilskin," she said. "What's the matter, you're so quiet? You'd think you had a world of troubles. Does your throat hurt you?"

Regina shook her head.

"Well, that's good news," Aunt Eileen said. "Go out and eat some of that ice cream. You've no business in here with your elders, bothering your head with what doesn't concern you. I have two quarts of ice cream out there, taking up space in my Frigidaire, and you've yet to stick a spoon in it. I wasn't offered ice cream on a silver platter when I was your age, I don't mind telling you. There's many the starving child would be glad of that ice cream."

Regina detached herself from the hassock and rounded the corner to the dining room. There she perched on the chair at the head of the table, the one with carved arms. The table's centerpiece was a round lake of mirror with a family of swans made out of salt floating motionlessly on it. Regina got up on her knees on the chair seat to lean in and breathe on the mirror. She printed in the vapor that appeared there the only word she knew—Regina— watched it fade, breathed again, wrote again.

"As I understand it," Mrs. Martin said in the living room, "she's no better than she should be and he's no better than she deserves."

"I saw the furniture going in," Aunt Eileen said. "She was flapping around like a duck in thunder, you'd have thought it was made of glass. She has her satisfactions. They say she has rugs you'd sink to your knees in them."

"I don't go for that antique hooey," Mrs. Martin said. "We had better in my poor papa's attic. I wouldn't set my foot across her door. I wouldn't touch clothes with her."

———

Moses Supposes

"No more would I," said Aunt Eileen, "but it makes me mad. There's my sister Rita as big as a house. Flat on her back in the midst of strangers, with her feet on a pillow and her prayer beads in her hand. And what thanks will she get in the end? No thanks. And God knows what the end will be. And there's that woman without an ounce of sense, married on a big mucky-muck in the building trades and enjoying life."

"Don't tell me it's the building trades," Mrs. Martin cautioned. "I wasn't born yesterday. It's something crooked, mark my words. And they fight like cats and dogs, as I understand it."

"Let them fight," said Aunt Eileen. "Don't tell me they fight. She's enjoying life . . . Regina!" she called. "Are you eating that ice cream?"

"Yep," Regina said, not moving.

"Did you slam the Frigidaire door, Regina?"

"Yep," Regina said. She got silently down from the chair and stretched out on the floor beneath the dining room table. She appraised the table's convoluted legs and its unfinished underparts and the highly polished unmarred mahogany leaf that was slung beneath it. There was a smell of Simoniz under there that in easier times she would have found invigorating.

She rolled out from under the table and looked at the world upside down. It looked queer, with the sideboard and the china closet hanging in the air, but no better.

"That's how I understand it," Mrs. Martin whispered noisily in the living room. "A stable boy. You remember the time her hobbyhorse threw her and she broke the both of her wrists? That's when it started. So they say."

"They say this and they say that," Aunt Eileen said

130

sourly, "but I don't care how you slice it, she's enjoying life."

"I wouldn't put it that way," Mrs. Martin said. "Shame wouldn't let me. She's no better than a common street-walker, if you want my honest opinion."

"I wouldn't have it for me or mine," Aunt Eileen said, in a tone that showed she could take or leave Mrs. Martin's honest opinion, "but she's seen a bit more than these four walls and that's all you'll see or I'll see till we see Saint Peter."

"Oh, Mother, that reminds me," Mrs. Martin said. "I'd better be off. If I don't have that man's lunch on the table, he'll have the streets up around me."

"Hughie's the same," Aunt Eileen said ritually. "Fetch and carry; carry and fetch."

Regina bent her knees and walked her feet, sliding her body flat along the floor to follow them, inch by inch, toward the kitchen. The scratchy, brilliant jungle on the dining room rug prickled and burned her through her sunsuit and up her naked shoulder blades. When she made it to the kitchen, the going was easier over the linoleum. Near the screen door to the back porch she hauled herself upright by the shapely iron leg of the sink. She let herself out onto the porch, taking pains not to let the screen door bang. Then she reeled across the porch and down the steps to the yard, noiselessly doing her drunk man imitation.

Once in the yard there was nothing to do. A shimmering moiré of heat hung low in the air. The grass was scorched, splashed with wilted dandelions, yellow as egg yolk, and a too-sweet foam of clover. The saw-toothed, cookie-shaped leaves of the hydrangea bushes were limp and blighted with the heat; the big puffy flower heads, ferociously blue

---

in the twilight, were bleached now, in the sun. The ground beneath the peach tree was littered with hard baby peaches, poisonously green. If you hammered them open, Regina knew, you found white baby pits that burst with a pop when you pinched them. The peach tree bled knobs of glossy topaz sap. They tasted exactly, Regina knew, like jujubes, only better. Sometimes they had ants in them, sometimes not. If you smashed the pit of a full-grown peach and ate the little almond that was in there, it would kill you, just like that.

Regina stopped to visit Shamrock, snoring in the doorway of her doghouse. Shamrock's nose worked, her toes spread, she flipped her tail and whined in her throat. She was having a terrible dream. Regina blew on Shamrock's whiskers. Shamrock stirred and grumbled and covered her eyes with her forepaws, like the monkey See-No-Evil. A beetle rowed out to the middle of Shamrock's water dish, foundered, drowned.

Regina ambushed the grape arbor and flung herself down underneath it, battering an elbow. The grass was lush and spiky in the arbor's puddled shade, but full of sharp stones, thrown there, with curses, by Regina's uncle Hughie, every time he mowed the lawn. She scouted around for an Indian paint-pot stone, but she didn't find one. A troubling, thrilling smell clung underneath the arbor, a dark, wild, lively smell like pulled-up weeds or Absorbine Jr. Regina breathed it, squinting through the grape leaves at the white sky. The robins snoozed in the apple tree, the climbing roses drooped along the fence. Regina's throat hurt. She was bitterly, violently lonesome. "You dope," she said to her mother in her mind. "You smelly dope. You double dope. You bustard."

———

In the hospital, diminished by insult and abandonment, Regina had dreamed of her mother. The edges of the dream had fused with the edges of disordered present fact and left her confused and grudge-bearing. She was mad at them all for what they had done to her, for the mystery and pain, the jail-barred crib they had put her in, the tapes that tied her to it, the cranky nurse who, wearing a baby's hat pinned to the top of her grown-up's head, sat all night in an isolation of green light beyond Regina's glass door. She was mad at them for the terrible plight of the little girl in the crib beside hers. That little girl's name was Marguerite and her leg had gotten broken—now how would they fasten it on again, how would they stick it on? When Regina had asked them, they'd laughed at her, and given her pineapple juice to drink. Regina's mother wouldn't have done that. Regina's mother knew Regina couldn't even stand to see anybody *else* drink pineapple juice, it was so nasty. But Regina's mother wasn't there.

Of all the horrors of the hospital, the dream, though, was the worst. God the Father had stood, in her dream, luminous in holy picture colors, at the top of the stairs in her own house in Locust Valley. He had a long beard and a halo and he carried a Little Play Doctor Kit. He looked down into the living room, where the water was rising. Regina's mother was down there in a rowboat. She lay on her back in the bottom of the boat, with her feet up on a seat, as she had one misty, half-remembered summer when they all went crabbing in the bay. The Phantom in his mask and his lavender tights was in the boat with her, but Regina wasn't there at all. The boat was leaking and the Phantom bailed and bailed with his hands, but the water kept rising. And then the windows of the living room turned into peepholes, little ones, then bigger ones, then huge ones, and the clear green burning water of Lake George poured in, full of starving black and silver fishes.

"You bustard," Regina said to her mother. How long did it take a lady to have a baby? Till Christmas? Till Easter? Till Regina's birthday? Till Regina started school? These occasions, variously proffered—as threats, as marvels, as bribes—were equally distant from her; they had no sequence and no likely, steady substance in her mind.

Regina ate a blade of grass. Her eyes brimmed with tears. She ignored them, let the ants walk over her, and listened to the growl of the bees. The grapes were all around her, hiding underneath the leaves, huddled up on one another like the stalks of unlaid eggs her mother found in roasting hens. Sometime—at the end of summer?—the grapes would swell and crack and turn a foggy purple. Between their sour skins and sour pulpy hearts lay an interval of musky juice. Regina's aunt Eileen made two things from the grapes: stiff bright purple jelly so sweet it made your nose run and a kind of smoky, tainted wine. A lot of the grapes would get mashed on the ground and the wasps would eat them.

Regina got to her hands and knees and crawled to the back of the arbor. She parted the grape leaves and crawled between them. The grape leaves looked as soft as suede, but they were rough when they touched you, like the tongue of a cat. Regina climbed the rustic fence into Mrs. Bederman's yard and cut around in back of Mrs. Bederman's bridal wreath bushes and out into Mrs. Bederman's street. Mrs. Bederman was listening to *Our Gal Sunday* on the radio and singing "All Alone by the Telephone," in a loud voice, with expression, to herself.

———

Regina skipped down Mrs. Bederman's block. Mrs. Bederman's voice followed her, working out a rather dirge-like arrangement of "The Love Bug Will Bite You If You Don't Watch Out." Regina crossed a street and entered an anonymous corner yard. A little boy puttering with a rock and a roll of exploding caps told her to get right out of there. Regina said she'd get out of there her eyeball. She ducked through a hole in Mrs. Crestlake's hedges and found herself in Mrs. Crestlake's yard. It was heavily planted and growing rank. The birdbath had no water in it, only some scum and a slimy skeletal leaf. The fish pool, made of pink cement, smelled like garbage.

It was in the wrong place, in the sun, Mrs. Crestlake had told her, and the water got hot and cooked most of the fish. When Mrs. Crestlake bought more fish for the pool, the two that were left, a black and a silver, ate them right up, and after that she had just surrendered on them; they had no morals, Mrs. Crestlake said, she didn't want any part of them. They were in there now, the black and the silver, brooding at the bottom of the murky water, quivering their gills and sniffing each other; they weren't even friends. The edges of the fish pool were seamed with tar, gummy and blistered from the sun. Regina impressed ten fingerprints in it before she went to knock on Mrs. Crestlake's back door. There was no answer. A wooden trellis, obscured by morning glories, arched over the back door. Regina sat down inside the trellis, on the milk box, to wait for Mrs. Crestlake. There were four coffee rings, in blue Dugan's boxes with cellophane windows, tied to Mrs. Crestlake's doorknob. There were two quarts of milk on the step. Regina got up and looked in the milk box. She saw two more quarts of milk and a carton of cottage cheese. She put the lid of the milk box down again and sat on it. She folded her hands on her knees and waited. After a while she heard water running in the house, so she got up and knocked very hard. Nothing happened, so she knocked again. After some really determined knocking, Mrs. Crestlake opened the door.

"All right, Buster," Mrs. Crestlake said. "What do *you* want?"

"I was operated," Regina said shyly, looking at the doorsill.

"Good for you," Mrs. Crestlake said. "What else is new?"

"You said I should come over," Regina said.

"I said that?" Mrs. Crestlake said. "I couldn't have said that. My judgment's too sound."

Regina looked up at her. Mrs. Crestlake was wearing a bedraggled black satin slip decorated with red rosebuds. Although she prided herself on being peppy, she neither looked nor sounded peppy today. And though she usually smelled overpoweringly wonderful, the aroma that rose from her was sour-sweet and ominous, reminding Regina of something boiled-over or spoiled. Regina picked up a quart of milk and tried to hand it to Mrs. Crestlake. "Leave it," Mrs. Crestlake said. "Leave *it, I said*. Let it rot. Come in if you're coming."

Regina followed Mrs. Crestlake into the kitchen. The kitchen was hot and very messy. Mrs. Crestlake's house was always messy and sometimes worse than messy. Once a bug walked right across the kitchen floor. Once a mouse had. Mrs. Crestlake had seen Regina's suffering-for-her face on the mouse occasion, and told Regina to forget it and pretend she was slumming. This, like almost everything else Mrs. Crestlake had ever said to her, struck Regina as unintelligible but hilarious.

"Fix yourself a drink," Mrs. Crestlake said. "If you want one. There's no ice." She sat down on the kitchen chair, feeling her way. Her knees came through a place at the bottom of her slip where the lace was separated from the hem. She took hold of the flounce and yanked it off, right around the slip, and sat there with the streamer of torn lace dangling from her hand. A flickering, undeveloped frown dissolved her features; it was as regular as the play of a searchlight. She felt on the floor for a teacup with her free hand, picked it up, and drank something from it.

Regina found a big Hoffman's cream-soda bottle in the refrigerator. Mrs. Crestlake's was the largest and most vacant refrigerator in Regina's experience. There was only a small amount of cream soda left, but the bottle had the cap on it. Regina couldn't find a clean glass in the cupboard, so she poured the cream soda into a teacup, like Mrs. Crestlake's. The cream soda was flat. She held onto the bottle cap.

"Let's beat it out of here, Buster," Mrs. Crestlake said. "Kitchens depress me."

They went into the living room, carrying their teacups. Everything in the living room was red or black or brilliant blue, and reminded Regina of the wrappers around packages of firecrackers and of the drilled coins that came in some of the packages. "Chinese Modern," Mrs. Crestlake had said to Regina, the first time Regina had been there, "isn't it nitsy?"

Mrs. Crestlake sprawled on the low red couch with the dragons and the frogs printed on it. Her ankles were crossed and her knees gapped apart. She wore an old pair of white fur mules, so broken-down and dirty that Regina was embarrassed to look at them. An enormous gong, like a big black saucer, was mounted on the wall above the couch, together with a leather-covered mallet to hit it with. Mrs. Crestlake reached up behind her for the mallet and gave the gong a halfhearted whack. She always did that when she sat there. She listened attentively to its faded bong, lolling her head against the couch. Regina sipped her cream soda, pressing the bottle cap against her upper arm to fake a vaccination.

"Are you looking at my roots?" Mrs. Crestlake said. She sounded slack and mopey. "Don't look at my roots, you." She laid the spread fingers of one hand on the crown of her head and at the same time tilted her head back to drain the teacup of whatever it was she'd been drinking. "Pretend I'm wearing a hat," she said more cheerfully. "Don't ask me what color, you realist. Pretend I'm wearing a big black hat. With feelers. How are you fixed for cash?"

"Excuse me?" Regina said.

"Oh, my God," Mrs. Crestlake said. "Another pauper. I might have known. Fair-weather friends. Sunshine patriots. I've had sufficient. Don't you think that's funny? 'I've had sufficient.' Pardon while I adjust my veil." She began to laugh in a breathless, uncontrollable way, but in a minute she was sad again and full of blame. "I've got pence none," she said. "How do you like that? Pence none. There is no gas in my car. There is no money in this house to *buy* gas. How do you like that? I *walked* up from the station this morning." She held the teacup upside down to prove to herself that it was empty. She gripped the arm of the couch and pushed herself upright. Holding herself very straight and walking with conspicuous grace, as though watched by a roomful of people, she crossed the black rug to a painted cabinet and threw open all its doors. A counter upholstered in patent leather sped out to meet her and a music box played "How Dry I Am." She cocked her head and conducted the tune with her forefinger, attempting to truck in time. "Wonderful, no?" she said to Regina. "They could really write music in those days. That was before people went bad." The shelves behind the counter and above it were heavily stocked with empty bottles, many of them lying on their sides. Mrs. Crestlake indicated them with a grand gesture, catching herself on the tip of the nose with her flailing hand. "Dead soldiers," Mrs. Crestlake said. "Wouldn't that bring a tear to your eye? Dead soldiers." She reached into the recesses of the cabinet and withdrew an exotic bottle, which she held up to the light. Three globes, each of them the shape of the mercury vial on a thermometer, melted into what appeared to be one partitioned neck. Red dregs lay in one of the globes; green dregs in another; the third was full of brown syrup. Mrs. Crestlake filled her teacup from the brown globe and took a grimacing swallow. "Crème de cacao," she said to Regina. "Ever taste it? Tastes like something you'd put on a rash. If you hated yourself. Tastes like something you'd put on somebody *else's* rash." She replenished the teacup and restored the bottle to its place, well back in the cabinet. "I have no money," Mrs. Crestlake said piercingly, facing the cabinet. "*No money.*"

"Ask your daddy," Regina said sensibly, drumming her heels on her chair.

"Annie doesn't live here anymore," Mrs. Crestlake said.

"Excuse me?" Regina said.

"He flew the coop," Mrs. Crestlake said. "As husbands go, he went."

"Whereabouts?" Regina asked warily, smiling to show that she knew she was being hoaxed.

"Wherever they go when they've had sufficient," Mrs. Crestlake said, laughing again. "He'd had sufficient. He looks me right in the eye—this eye, see it—he looks me right in the eye—historical present—and he says, 'Vivian,' he says, 'Vivian, enough is too much, Vivian, and I've had sufficient.' He's the sort of person that says things like that just as if they meant something. He stands there with his thumbs in the armholes of his invisible vest and he says, 'Vivian,' he says, 'Vivian, I've had sufficient.' And you know what I said? Did I laugh: I said, '*My name is not Vivian.*'"

"Vivian is so," Regina said.

"You remind me of him," Mrs. Crestlake said. "A couple of realists. Two know-it-alls. He calls himself a realist. He's got a big round rock where his heart should be, that's his trouble. You know what he said to me? He said, 'I'm through wiping your chin.' Can you imagine, anybody saying that to me, of all the lovely people? Oh, he's sterling, he really is." She took a handbag made of multicolored wooden beads from an end table, clicked it open, and turned its contents out on the rug. Lipsticks scurried every which way. Regina rushed to capture them.

"Leave 'em lay," Mrs. Crestlake ordered. "Something for the sweeper." She went down on one knee to sort through the welter of junk on the rug—tattered scraps of paper with pencil writing on them, a key chain strung with more charms than keys, an enameled compact, some kernels of corn that Regina knew were used for marking Bingo cards, a handful of shabby-looking milk of magnesia tablets, all of it sifted over with an ugly dust of face powder. She uncovered a nickel and held it out between her thumb and forefinger. "There's what I have between me and God," Mrs. Crestlake said. "Wouldn't that bring a tear to your eye? A five-cent piece. You want it? It's yours." She seized Regina's hand in both of hers, smacked the nickel into her palm, and folded Regina's unwilling fingers over it.

"No thank you," Regina said properly. She put her fist on the coffee table and gently deposited the nickel there.

Mrs. Crestlake slapped the coin and dashed it off the table. It fell at the heel of Regina's left sandal. Regina stooped to pick it up and the little gold medal she wore around her neck swung out from under the bib of her sunsuit. Mrs. Crestlake caught it and held it so that Regina couldn't straighten up.

"What's that for?" Mrs. Crestlake demanded. She sounded shrewd. "For luck?"

Regina shook her head. "For luck is a rabbit foot," she said.

"Izzatso?" Mrs. Crestlake said meanly. "It never brought much luck to the rabbit. Did you ever think of that?"

"No," Regina said, appalled.

"Do you say prayers?" Mrs. Crestlake asked. "Let's hear you say one."

Regina shook her head, blushing. Her neck hurt her from bending over.

"Come on, Buster, I haven't got all day."

Regina took a deep breath and coasted downhill on it. "There are four posts upon my bed upon each post an an-

---

gel spread Saints Matthew Mark Luke and John God bless the bed that I lay on amen."

"Well, isn't that lovely," Mrs. Crestlake said. "Unfortunately, I don't have four posts on my bed. There's nothing on my bed but a boudoir doll. I have a Hollywood bed and there are no damn posts on it *at* all."

"Oh," Regina said. She didn't know what to do about that.

Mrs. Crestlake released the medal, picked up the nickel, and thrust it at Regina. "Take that," she insisted. "Put it in your pocket. Put it in your hope chest. Buy yourself a ride on the subway. *I've* already *had* a ride on the subway." She raised her head and assumed an expression of synthetic profundity. "There's poetry in that," she said. " 'I've already had a ride on the subway.' Boy, what he could do with that."

Regina dropped the nickel in her pocket. "I better go home now," she said. "Thank-you-very-much-for-a-very-nice-time."

"No you don't, Buster," Mrs. Crestlake said. "Sit down."

Regina sat down.

Mrs. Crestlake used both hands to scoop up the compact and the other things and dump them on the coffee table. Then she struggled to her feet, fetched the bottle of crème de cacao from the cabinet, and returned to sit by Regina on the couch. As she seated herself, she broke into song. She had a strident, oddly pleasing voice, but she startled Regina badly. "I don't care if it rains or freezes," she sang, "I am safe in the arms of Jesus. I am Jesus' little lamb; yes, by Jesus Christ, I am." She turned on Regina as if to strike her. "Do you like that?"

"*I* don't know," Regina said.

"You don't know much," Mrs. Crestlake said. "Or you wouldn't be living in a town like this one. One time I sang that in Sunday school and I got walloped for it."

"*I* don't live here," Regina said, affronted. "I live in Locust *Valley*."

"Same difference," Mrs. Crestlake said. She picked up her compact from the coffee table and stared hard at herself in its mirror. What she saw there seemed not to move her much one way or the other. "I look like I got hit with a pig bladder." She scrubbed her face with the flat grimy powder puff. Perspiration sparkled on her neck and shoulders and in the cove between her speckled, faintly lavender breasts. "They're animals," she said. "Remember that. Let them crawl to you, and keep on smiling, but don't lift a finger to do them any good—'yes, dear; sure, honey; yes, yes, yes' "—she touched the catch of the rouge compartment and stroked rouge along her cheekbones—"but all the time you say to yourself, 'I'll see you in hell first'—that's the way to do it." She reached out and dabbed Regina's nose with the rouge puff. "You hear me?" Regina laughed, flinching. Mrs. Crestlake swabbed Regina's nose again, leaving a coral blot there. "Your mother's calling you," she said, discarding the compact and pouring herself some more crème de cacao.

"No, she isn't," Regina said. "My mommy's in Lake George."

"Lake George," Mrs. Crestlake said. "I'd as soon be in a cemetery. Get everything in your name, that's another thing. Don't trust them. They won't trust you. Or even if they do, that's beside the point. But they won't. Even Nutsy Fagan in the deli—I did a lot of trade in that deli—

---

you think he'd cash me a little bit of an insignificant fifteen-dollar check? Don't make me laugh. And Delucci in the package store—the money I've seen me spend in there—he hides in the back when he sees me coming, rotating his big brown eyes; he sends the kid out. 'The manager's not here today,' the kid says. 'I haven't got the authority.' Some manager. Some authority. 'I haven't got the authority.' What a broken record. So I swep' out. He was in there telling fairy stories, my sterling husband. He thinks it's money, but it isn't money. What do I care about money? Am I the gold-digging kind? No, I just want to stick him where he's tender. He's rock, all but the pocketbook. Even that doesn't hurt *enough*. Nothing I do to hurt him hurts him, that's how much he cares about me. There was a time back there when I was perfect, but he doesn't see things that way anymore. Buster, there's a lot I could tell you about human nature. Anything you want to know, just ask me."

"Did you ever have any little babies?" Regina asked her.

"Oh, stop the *melodrama!*" Mrs. Crestlake said, putting her feet up on the coffee table.

"Thank-you-very-much-for-a-very-nice-time," Regina said, standing up.

"I love him more than the day I married him," Mrs. Crestlake said. "Imagine my surprise."

Regina went out through the kitchen and home the way she had come, running. When she got to the corner, she threw the nickel down a grating in the gutter. Once a shining screaming cat had hidden in there, after a car had broken its jaw. A policeman had come with his gun and shot it. Regina and her aunt Eileen had cried, but some of the children had thought it was funny. Regina ran faster. When she

———

was back in her aunt Eileen's yard, Regina sat on the porch steps, panting. Her aunt Eileen came up the driveway, fixed up to go out. She had a hairbrush in her hand, and she was beside herself with anger.

"I've been shouting my head off on you this last half hour and you never thought it worth your while to answer me," she said, pulling barrettes from Regina's hair. "Stand up there. Look at that head, a mass of tats; merciful God, you're all in a sweat, you've been running like a redshank in this broiling sun and you just over an operation. Where were you anyway, and me black in the face with calling you?"

"No place," Regina said. The brush caught in her long snarled hair and snapped her head back against Aunt Eileen's breasts. "Is that *chalk* on your face?" Aunt Eileen said, tilting up Regina's chin. "It is chalk. Merciful God, you'll be the death of me." She steered Regina up the steps and into the kitchen. She began to work on her with Ivory soap but changed her mind and brought instead, from the buffet drawer where she kept her damask tablecloths from Ireland, a box containing three soap flowers, each one a different color and each with a different perfume. She told Regina to choose which one she wanted but to hurry up about it. Regina picked the blue one. Aunt Eileen lathered the scented soap and scrubbed Regina's face and ears and knees and elbows with it, and bullied her into a clean sun-suit. "I have to get to the bank before it closes," Aunt Eileen said, pulling off one of Regina's socks. "I have to get to the post office."

"I can dress *myself*," Regina said, hopping on one foot, scowling.

"Never mind that," Aunt Eileen said. "Other foot now.

That's it. I have to get to Bohacks. I have to get to Aunt
Mary Ann's and pin up a couple of hems for her. Hughie's
dinner's in the Frigidaire; he has patients all the evening
anyhow. We'll eat with Aunt Mary Ann and Jack. Pray God
it isn't salmon loaf as usual. Let's see your teeth. They'll do.
Come on now."

·   ·   ·

When Aunt Eileen guided the DeSoto up Meridian Street
late that night, Regina was slumped, nine-tenths asleep,
against her shoulder. Aunt Eileen negotiated the corner of
her own street apprehensively, appearing as she always did
crouched at the wheel, grim and unresourceful. She kept
one nervous eye on the road and one on Regina; she was in
terror of having to make a short stop that would send her
passenger hurtling through the windshield. She was
halfway past Mrs. Crestlake's house before she noticed anything. Then she gasped and began to back up. Regina's eyes
slid open. Mrs. Crestlake's house was lit with floodlights.
Her hedges were partly knocked down. The whole side wall
of the house, toward the rear, where the kitchen was, had
disappeared. Sheets of what looked like black tar paper lay
all over the lawn, and the black wreck of the kitchen chair
was upended in the driveway. There was so much water,
you'd have thought it had been raining. People eddied on
the churned-up lawn, collecting in clots, dispersing, coming
together again. They talked in low, excited voices, setting
each other straight, and some of them were laughing. The
two little Bederman boys, out way past their bedtime,
played touch tag between the bric-a-brac bushes until a
man from the volunteer fire department, done up in a yel-

low slicker, stopped them. The pink plaster one-legged bird and the silver-green ball on its stand were just where they had always been. Regina, clouded, drugged with sleep, thought it looked like the parish bazaar on the lawn at night at St. Brendan's. The car went forward, with a grinding lurch, stalled, went forward. Uncle Hughie bounded out of the house as the car pulled into the driveway.

"My God, Eileen, it was terrible! You missed it. It was terrible! I was the one that called the department."

"That Mary Ann, her tongue goes like a hand bell," said Aunt Eileen, in the thin, silly voice of catastrophe. "Carry that child, she's dead with sleep. What happened, anyhow?"

"The Dutch act," Uncle Hughie said. "I thought it was a cherry bomb, it rattled the glass in the windows. The Bederman boys set a cherry bomb off in an oil can, not a half an hour before. I had old man King in the chair at the time and he nearly jumped over the moon. So I thought it was a cherry bomb. Then I said to myself, 'That was no cherry bomb,' and I run into the street without my coat on. And the place was burning! Her head in the oven. My God, she brought it off all right. The Dutch act."

"God pity her," Aunt Eileen said fervently, "she'll be in hell before morning."

"It was terrible," Uncle Hughie said. He was pulling and tugging at Regina, trying to fold her up in his arms and extract her from the cramped front seat without harm. He staggered across the moonlit yard with Regina in his arms. Her head bounced on his shoulder and her boneless legs kicked against his knees, getting in his way. "Get the doors, Eileen," he called. He was huffing and puffing when he got to the stairway. He stopped a minute, shifting Regina, hoisting her higher in his arms, kissing her cheeks.

———

"You're a slippery fish, old Reggie," he said. "You're my slippery fish." Regina smiled and went to sleep with her nose against the bristles of his neck.

· · ·

When she opened her eyes, it was nearly lunchtime and the dark green sleep-shades were down to the sills of the three big windows in her room. Her aunt Eileen and her uncle Hughie were by the window that looked out into the street. Her uncle Hughie sat in the slipper chair, drinking a cup of tea. His back was to the window. Aunt Eileen was settled on the edge of his chair, but she faced the street; she was peeking out around the shade. "Where did they find him at last, Hughie?" she asked her husband softly. He said he didn't know. "You know, all right," Aunt Eileen said. "And I know more than what's good for me. I saw him myself in the early hours of morning, with his hammer and his nails and his hothouse flowers. A fat lot of good they'll do her now. He was just risen out of a drunken sleep, or I'm a lot more wrong than I'm used to being."

"Ah, now, Eileen," Uncle Hughie said, "don't think about it."

"I'm going, Hughie," said Aunt Eileen.

"You're not," Uncle Hughie said, quite loud, and she shushed him. "The thing's to be held this afternoon, and by tomorrow it'll all be over," he said. "Put it out of your mind like a sensible woman."

"What thing?" she said, frowning.

"The funeral," Uncle Hughie said reluctantly. "The cremation."

"Cremation!" Aunt Eileen said. "Merciful God. 'Here's

———

148

your hat, what's your hurry.' There's more wickedness in the world than you can shake a stick at."

Regina got out of bed and crept up on them. Uncle Hughie saw her and put his finger to his lips, pointing with his thumb for her to scare her aunt Eileen. Regina jumped on her and tickled her to make her squeal.

"Go on, you wild Indian," Aunt Eileen said, laughing. "We thought you'd sleep your life away. I could murder that Mary Ann with her gab, keeping us out till all hours." She pulled up the shade on the window and Regina looked out. She saw Mrs. Crestlake's house, familiar and strange. A big bouquet of flowers, white ones, tied with broad glistening white and violet ribbons, was fastened to the door beside the knocker. A policeman sat on the step beneath it, smoking a cigarette.

"Tell that man to throw away his dirty cigarette," Aunt Eileen said indignantly. "Tell him I'll report him. It's not decent, Hughie. Go you and tell him that."

"I will not," Uncle Hughie said.

"Whereabouts did Mrs. Crestlake go when her house exploded?" Regina asked her uncle Hughie, leaning on his knees. She was not surprised by what had happened, only by the machinery of things.

"She went to sing with the angels," Uncle Hughie said uncomfortably. "It was a terrible accident that happened, Regina, and God took her."

"God or the devil," said Aunt Eileen.

"Will you make up your mind whose side you're on?" Uncle Hughie said. "You give me the head staggers."

"You think you know hell and all just because you're a professional man," Aunt Eileen said, getting mad.

"Does she know a lot of songs?" Regina asked. "Does

———

she know 'All Alone by the Telephone'? Does she know 'Froggy Went A-courtin'?" It seemed to her there were a lot of questions she wanted to ask, but she couldn't think what they were. She wondered how Mrs. Crestlake would sound singing "Froggy Went A-courtin," but that was her mother's song and she didn't think Mrs. Crestlake would sing it right. She wondered if Mrs. Crestlake had said good-bye to Turk and the fishes after her house exploded and why her relatives had not taken her, instead of God, and how long she would stay away. "When will she come back?" she asked her uncle Hughie, butting her head against his chest. He smelled of Florida Water.

"I'm going, Hughie," Aunt Eileen said. "And Regina's going with me. There's no reason to wrap her in cotton wool. That's what Dennis and Rita do, and it's nothing to their credit. She's got to live in the world, she's got to learn about it. And she'll never learn younger."

"Get down off your soapbox," Uncle Hughie said. "Have you no sense? She's only a bit of a baby."

"Going where?" Regina asked.

"To the Chapel Funeral Home," Aunt Eileen said distantly. "To visit that lady across the street that passed away. It's only as if she was sleeping, Reggie, it's nothing to be afraid of." But she looked afraid herself, as she had the afternoon she'd taken Regina to the hospital.

They were fooling her, Regina thought. You could be singing or you could be sleeping, but you couldn't be singing and sleeping both. "I don't want to," she said.

"Nobody asked you what you wanted," Aunt Eileen said. "Mind your beeswax."

·   ·   ·

———

She gave Regina her lunch and supervised her dressing. Regina wore her navy blue dress with the white crocheted collar and her leghorn hat with the grosgrain ribbons down the back. At the last minute, Aunt Eileen, who was fitted out in a black Bemberg sheer, lip pomade, and a varnished straw skimmer, made Regina take her hat off and heated the tongs in the gas flame to give her a few more curls. Uncle Hughie hung around muttering. Aunt Eileen kept thinking of things to do to Regina to make her more presentable. "Is this a wake or a wedding?" Uncle Hughie said at last, nearly as red as his wife. Aunt Eileen breathed fire at him, jammed Regina's hat on her head, and towed her out onto the back porch by her white-gloved hand.

She told Regina to wait there while she backed out the car. Regina waited, admiring the celluloid Scottie dog glued to the flap of her powder blue purse. Then, without warning to herself, she began to cry. Aunt Eileen opened the garage doors, got into the car, gunned the motor, and got out again. She came back and told Regina to go inside and take off her clothes and lie down on her bed like a good girl, she looked very tired. Throughout this speech, she kept her gaze no higher than Regina's ankles. When she raised it, she saw with awful remorse that Regina had been crying long enough to reach the anguished, pop-eyed stage. Regina wailed that she *wouldn't* lie down, she'd been lying down all *night*. Aunt Eileen said to do as she was told or she'd be very, very sorry she hadn't. Aunt Eileen watched her go into the house and then got back in the car. Inside, Uncle Hughie stripped Regina to the skin within a minute. Regina sat in the middle of her bed, on top of the spread, in her underpants, not crying now, but fuming mad. Uncle Hughie watched out the window of the up-

---

stairs hall, keeping behind the organdy curtains.

Regina heard the sound of the motor running and the sputtering gravel as the car backed partway down the driveway. Then the gravel noises stopped, but the motor went on. Then the motor stopped and there were only the scattered, widely spaced, faraway reports of firecrackers. The car was still in the driveway. Uncle Hughie hurried in and sat down on Regina's bed. "She's coming," he said. "Now, don't you say a word."

Aunt Eileen bustled up the stairs, very flustered. She was already pulling her dress off over her head. "I've never turned my word on you yet, Hughie," she said righteously; "in all the years we've been married, I've never gone against your wishes. And I won't do it now. Lie down, Regina."

Regina lay down.

"It's just that she had nothing and no one, Hughie," Aunt Eileen said. "I've got to get these corsets off, they're killing me. There's nobody belonging to her. She hadn't a friend in the street."

"That won't bother her now," Uncle Hughie said.

"If it was me, it would bother me," said Aunt Eileen. She sat down by Regina's head, fidgeting her smooth, worn hands in the lap of her lacy slip—a Mother's Day present from Uncle Hughie. "And she put me in mind of someone, Hughie. God forgive me, but it's true. She put me in mind of Rita—she wouldn't have been more than Rita's age— Rita was blond when she was little like Reggie. She put me in mind of her somehow. Did she you?"

"Not a bit of it," Uncle Hughie said. "A bold piece of goods like that one was. You're daffy."

"Maybe I am," Aunt Eileen said. She turned her wedding

———

ring around and around in the groove it had worn for itself in her finger. "I don't know what to do to do the right thing."

"I'll tell you something," Uncle Hughie said. "But don't go broadcasting it around the doors and spilling it to all your cronies. She'd put his name to a pile of checks, among some other shenanigans, and he was set to have the law on her."

"Oh, he'd never've done it, would he, though? She was his wife after all."

"She was and she wasn't," Uncle Hughie said, "and she'd done him out of a good bit of money. And two years or five years put away is forever when it's standing there looking at you."

"Lord have mercy on her," Aunt Eileen said. "She had no right doing what she did. Lord have mercy on her; she had no damn business doing it."

"How long is two years?" Regina asked, sighing.

"Why aren't you asleep?" Aunt Eileen demanded. "Didn't I get through telling you to go to sleep. How high is up? Now, go asleep and don't be bothering me." She made a face of warning at her husband as she adjusted Regina's head on the pillow and straightened out her arms and legs. "Do you love me, ladybug?" she asked Regina meekly.

"I guess so," Regina said.

"Give us a kiss, then," Aunt Eileen said, leaning over her. Regina threw her arms around Aunt Eileen's neck and kissed her energetically.

"God forgive me, look what I've done," Aunt Eileen groaned. "I've got paint on the face of that innocent child. Ah God, that strikes me as awful."

———

"Wipe it off and stop your noise," Uncle Hughie said.

Aunt Eileen lifted the tail of her slip and rubbed the lipstick off Regina's jaw. "I'd have given my eyes for a child of my own," she whispered, ready to cry. "Do you know that, Hughie?"

"Now wait, Eileen," Uncle Hughie said, "you had the two little girls of your own, and that's more than is given to many a woman."

"And they died before they lived," Aunt Eileen said. "Do you never think about them?"

"That's all over with years ago," Uncle Hughie said. "You mustn't let it work on your mind."

"Maybe they're better off," Aunt Eileen said somberly. "It's a dog's life, a woman's life. I wouldn't wish it on a dog."

"Are you sick or what ails you?" Uncle Hughie said. "Did I leave the cap off the milk bottle or the cover off the garbage can or what did I do?"

"You didn't do anything," Aunt Eileen said, not looking at him, playing with Regina's hair. "You're a good man, Hugh. You've been good to me. You're better than I deserve."

"Jesus Murphy, you are sick," Uncle Hughie said. "Look at you in your big black petticoat. You make my blood roar. You're a scandal to the jaybirds." He pinched Aunt Eileen's flat black satin buttock, and she swatted at his hand.

"Stop that you, what's got into you? Broad daylight and in front of the child." She moved Regina over and lay down by her side. "Go away, you devil, and let us get our rest. We've got a big night tonight, if God spares us. It's the Fourth. Uncle Hughie's bought a grand big box of fireworks. What all did you get, Hughie?"

———

"Roman candles," Uncle Hughie said. "Sparklers. Sky rockets. Cherry bombs. The whole caboodle."

"Oh Hughie?" Aunt Eileen said suddenly. "Do you think it would be decent? With a death in the street?"

"Shut up, Eileen, for the love of God," Uncle Hughie said. "You'd drive any man distracted." He lay down beside Aunt Eileen on the bed and put his arm around her and Regina.

"You can stop the familiarity," Aunt Eileen said. "It's hotter than the hinges of hell." She yawned. "We've got a big night tonight, if God spares us."

Regina moved her head on the pillow. She knew, without knowing, that God spares no one. When she shut her eyes, she saw her mother. Floating, floating, pale and swollen, underneath the surface of the queer green water of Lake George. Floating, floating, sleeping, singing, smiling at the moon. The fishes glided over her, black and silver fishes, and slashed at her with needle teeth and tangled in her hair. Regina made a little noise of outrage and thudded her heels on the bed. "I don't know what I'm *lying* here for," she said grumpily.

"You go asleep or I'll take a switch to you," said Aunt Eileen.

———

Exit
Interview

"Twice a week since God was young you told me you're leaving your wife," says Elizabeth Lutz, deviling Bud Heally on the Metroliner. "And you didn't leave her."

"There are strategic issues at issue, Lutzy," Bud Heally says. "Tactics. Logistics. But I'm leaving her, the bitch," says lying Bud Heally, who tenderly loves his ruin of a wife, his houseful of irritating children. "Threw a shoe at her this morning."

Elizabeth blows steamboat toots across the mouth of her green glass pony of white wine. "Shoe at her," she says, crooning and hooting across the mouth of the bottle. "Shoe-oo-oo."

Elizabeth has large clear eyes of an unorthodox coppery color. Her effervescent hair is reddish, too; it sparkles. Her eyebrows and lashes are black and seem to Bud adroitly placed. Newness and freshness shoots out from her in dangerous vapors and in rays.

"Elizabeth," Bud says, "if you didn't work for me, you wouldn't give me the time of day. You wouldn't even be sitting next to me on this train."

Elizabeth bugs her fine eyes. She puts her pony down on the seat-back tray and pooches out her perfect lips and flutters them with a forefinger.

He notices again the only imperfection of her person. Her fingernails are thick and plastic-looking, owing, he supposes, to some malady. Bravely, she keeps them long and spade-shaped and paints them unremarkable pale colors. The way she uses her hands wrings his heart; she is deft, but she makes odd mandarin accommodations to favor her long, ugly, possibly painful fingernails. Seeing her do this produces in him mysterious licks and flickers of feeling, and once in a dream he removed from her this disfigurement, this enchantment, this curse of animal claws. Her mutilated fingertips, free, tapped out a stipple of bloody prints on the untraveled flesh of his body.

"Lutzy," he says, "what are your thoughts on the client meeting? Pretty hairy meeting, am I right? Or maybe I'm not right, give me the unvarnished."

He has dropped his voice so the art director and the writer, confabbing two seats in front of them, won't overhear and come back to hassle him some more about the meeting, in the course of which he sold them down the river. He is hoping a little that Elizabeth will tell him the client meeting wasn't so bad, or that he, personally, did an awfully good job, but neither of these things is so and he doubts that Elizabeth will attempt them. He feels a kind of aftershock of shame about the meeting. There was a time when he could handle any meeting, save it, bend it to his purpose, win the client over, make the meeting pay. He could do those things without thinking about them, thinking about several other things, the newspaper he'd once thought he'd like to run in a small town in Maine, the bed and breakfast and bait shop his wife once yearned for in Oregon, his oldest kid's soccer game, his next-oldest kid's afternoon at the Enrichment Center, his other kid's having to use a crutch for a while and hating it, his newest kid getting ready to be born. Or just what his wife was probably cooking for dinner and whether he'd make love to her afterward, big as she was and hilariously horny.

He is now hard put to think about anything. Barely able to remember why they gather for these meetings in big solemn expensively appointed conference rooms. Because Bud Heally needs the money. Desperately needs the money, he is able to remember that.

"They peed all over us," Elizabeth says.

"They did what?" He is startled, over and over again, by the mouths on these lovely, carefully raised, elegantly educated young women. "Asshole," he has heard one dewy, polished, scarily accomplished junior say to her recent husband on the telephone, "don't shit me, you fucker, you know what I'm saying? You suck." Depending from her neck at the time was a strand of diamonds and sapphires. He knows this, because, believing it was a string of sparkly cheap stuff, he stared. He wondered why her father, a man described by her as "a farmer," but a man, it turns out, who farms rice—rice—for fun, but owns most of California, didn't bring her up to know that rhinestones were for evening, a point Bud's mother impressed upon him when he was dating. It was a way to tell the ladies from the tramps. Also, of course, he was staring because he liked to study the slopes of the rice farmer's daughter's considerable breasts, an interest she noted quickly and commented upon with amusement and favor. She has loudly and merrily pointed out that Bud summons her to his office on chilly days just for the notorious pleasure of watching her enormous nipples stiffen.

Bud likes all this, or he thinks he likes it; he likes it, it makes the time go by, but he is prim. He wouldn't like it for Elizabeth or for his wife or for his several daughters. He is fair-skinned and a little fat and he blushes agonizingly, like a woman in the change. His wife used to talk quite freely and funnily to him about sex, but only when they were by themselves, alone. Now she is obliged to talk about things more intimate and frightening than sex and they are never alone; death is with them.

"You're right," Bud says, "they peed all over the creative." They peed on more than the creative, but he is not yet prepared to admit that he has personally been peed upon. "Good creative, too," he says dutifully.

"Was it?" Elizabeth says. "I thought it was dumb."

"Me, too," Bud says. "Too goofy. This business is really all just moving goods out of warehouses. It's all the guy holds up the box and says, 'Buy this, turkey.' The sonnet form it's not. Tap dancing it's not. Though I like tap dancing."

———

"When the client looks at you, he says, 'Is this funny? Explain to me why this is funny.' That was the part of the meeting I hated," Elizabeth says.

"Explain to me why this is funny, you sad ass."

"I thought you were going to hit him."

"Right," Bud says. First he thought he was going to hit the client, then he thought he was going to lick his shoes, if the client happened to fancy having his shoes licked.

"When I was starting out," Bud says, "I just loved the creative. The first ad I had anything to do with, it was wonderful. NOW THOUSANDS RUN UPHILL. All type, back of the book; black, greasy. For a truss."

Then he starts to tell her about his glory days, hard-charging, fire-breathing, heavy-hitting Bud Healy, on glamorous, big ticket accounts. But these are just war stories; she has heard them. It is no longer possible to recapture the fun of those days, the tales have all gone puerile, flat, and tinny.

"Lutzy," he says, "we're going to have to massage this Call Report, that meeting was a small bit hairy. We've got to save it for the record, bind up our wounds. Call Reports can be, you know, dangerous. Return to haunt you."

"Cover our fucking asses," Elizabeth says, laughing. "Save our bacon."

Elizabeth has a yellow legal-sized pad on her knee and she's been scribbling on it. Inscribed already in the mandated way, in her curiously back-listing social secretary hand—he thinks of it as rich girl handwriting—is the beginning of a Call Report. Present for the Client: So-and-so. Present for the Agency: Charles ("Bud") Healy, Account Supervisor; Elizabeth Lutz, Assistant Account Executive. There is no Account Executive for Elizabeth Lutz to assist at the moment, the Account Executive having been excused from his duties for a time to facilitate his recovery from Substance Abuse.

Bud doesn't mind filling in on this account. A politically correct account, it involves aquaculture, in this case, the farming of catfish. Oh, he *minds*—it's a nickel-and-dime account and fraught with troubles, one of them the fact that the clients are brothers, jealous, vain, and fumbling— but he needs the business, any business. He has been asked off his last account, a respectably billing candy bar account. The client said, literally and unashamedly, having just read a book, that Bud lacked "fire in the belly." Bud has perilously little business against which to charge his time. He is on the skids.

Any day now, the phone will ring and he will be summoned to the office of the affable, impersonal, hired-for-the-purpose ax, the blood-letter. This man will deliver a sheaf of material printed out on the agency's overdesigned letterhead, in case you forgot who was firing you. The stuff will be legal, impenetrable, and full of dopey typos because who really gives a shit. It will offer zip. It will give you what the law says the company has to give. The ax will want to shake your hand and tell you it was nice knowing you and that this episode, painful as it may seem, will turn out to be your eureka! experience.

The ax will mention with a confidential, a conspiratorial smile, any cherished sappy fantasy you have incautiously imparted to your friends and trusted colleagues. Maybe you should edit a country newspaper. Maybe you should run a rural bait shop. Aims and ambitions, the ax will tell you, he harbors himself. He will shoulder-punch you, point out that you are perhaps not totally committed to

———

161

"this crazy business of ours." He will say this with a noble swagger, as though the advertising business were a life-threatening adventure with humanitarian, even holy, risks and gains.

He will convey the clear though coded message that to sue the company is to render yourself forever unemployable. Over, out. The exit interview. Your ass is grass.

"I grant you that catfish farming is good for the globe," Bud says. "But am I wrong, or do these aquaculture guys even look like catfish?"

"Whiskery little boogers," Elizabeth says, writing on her pad. "Bottom feeders. Eat 'em, taste of mud. Used to catch 'em catfish with mah daddy."

"Yeah, you did," Bud says. "At—where would it be these days? Wherever the in-crowd is circling its wagons."

"Cleaned me many a mess of them boogers. Lop off they haids, peel 'em. Fry they asses in bacon grease."

"Lutz," Bud says warningly. He has no grasp on taste or correctness, political or otherwise. But he is scared of the art director, who is elegant, indolent, and black. He is afraid that Elizabeth's playful Mammy Yokum accent will offend, affront, or hurt the feelings of the art director, who may mistake it for an attempt at black street talk. The art director himself being in no position to know, since he has a British accent, a real British accent, not an anxiety neurosis. The client fools and the agency fools have, of course, assigned this exquisite young man to this account on the assumption that there is some mysterious affinity between black people and fish with whiskers. The art director has their number, but he is a tricky customer himself, though also easily brought to tears.

"Little cornmeal don't hurt nothing," Elizabeth Lutz

says. For all he knows, she is dating the art director, everybody else is. "You think I suffer from questionable taste?" she asks him. "You think I'd recognize questionable taste if it poked me in the gut? I don't," she says fondly. "But I personally majored in questionable taste at Sophie Newcomb, where I also minored in eye makeup."

"You have a marketing major from NYU," says Bud, who knows, "and an MBA from Wharton."

To his dismay, she seems upset. "So you know everything about me," she says, and her coppery eyes look full to overflowing.

"No, hell," Bud says. He thinks of his puzzling wife, his unknowable daughters. "I'm your supervisor, that's all. I read your jacket, forget it, who cares?"

This beautiful girl is acting as though a marketing degree from NYU, an MBA from Wharton, were a blot on her escutcheon, a disfigurement of her credentials, an armed robbery in her past, a strangled baby: He loves her.

"Lutzy," he says, "it'll just be between you and me."

"Go," she says. "You say that, then you noise it around. Love your suit."

She has hurt him. It's a terrible suit, an expensive mistake he has no option but to wear. The cut is wrong; European, dapperish, it makes him dumpy. The fabric, designed for the longest of hauls, is faintly but fiercely overplaided in a color known in Bud's old neighborhood as Polish blue. In the suit Bud looks, just slightly, as though he'd been gift wrapped. "Hell," he says, "it covers my nakedness, as my daddy used to say. My daddy ate mackerel, he didn't feature catfish."

"I do love your suit," Elizabeth says. "I love your suit. I love your eyes. You have the most beautiful eyes."

———

He is afraid of her, suddenly. She reminds him of his oldest daughter's golden kitten, warm and dead on his neighbor's lawn, not a mark on it, but all its works burst. Struck by a car? Or beaten to death with a baseball bat as his neighbor has boasted? "My mother used to say my eyes looked to her like two holes burned in a blanket," he says to Elizabeth. His mother did used to say that and it filled him, as a child, with guilt and anticipatory dread, not that his mother knew that. It doesn't do much for Elizabeth, one way or the other.

"Make you laugh," she says. "Jokelet." She hands him her yellow pad.

On the pad is the beginning of her Call Report. On her pad are the words *Hairy meeting*. The letters have been turned into people, the people at the meeting, and they are decorated with abundant hair, much of it pubic. The likenesses are extraordinary; Elizabeth has a talent or a gift. The figure that represents Bud is tellingly, touchingly, sheltered from much scrutiny—it is discreetly encumbered by distracting visual aids: charts, overhead projector, slide carousel. It is also idealized, young, slim. It has beautiful eyes. The figure that represents Elizabeth has full breasts and too long a neck. Here and there on the page are words of Bud's—"Bunch of stupid catfish farmers"; "Even look like catfish, hairy bastards"; "Peed all over the creative." These words have similarly been turned into recognizable people and made to grow great reels of riotous hair.

Bud is seized with a flaring feeling of oddly erotic betrayal. His face flames, his chest hurts with anger.

"*Christ*," he says to Elizabeth. People in the club car turn to look at them. He has seized her wrist and shakes it; her hand with the ugly painted nails flaps loosely. "What are

164

you doing to me?" Bud says. "What are you trying to do? I *need* this job." And then it is over. He drops her wrist and her hand falls like an object into her lap.

Bud's wife lies dying. She is shrinking. Shrinking, dying, she is almost four inches shorter than she was a year ago. She is dwindling, she is dying. Her bones have turned to honeycomb, to eaten coral. Her pelvis in the X ray looks like a vandalized road sign at a lonely crossroads. Blasted. Target practice. Brave and vengeful, wigged and terrified, Bud's wife stumbles on her walker toward the grave. Bud stumbles with her. She cannot sleep unless he lies beside her. He cannot, in her bed, succumb to sleep. He is afraid he will throw a leg across her, as he has done so many times across their span of years. He is afraid sometimes that he will seize her in his arms. Her bones then will crumble, will powder. He will hold filet of wife. Boneless slab of former girl. Human being, boned and rolled, ready for the fire.

His eyes drop to the piece of yellow paper. It is nothing. Prankish, kiddish, larky, dumb. This Lutz is harmless as a child, he thinks. But his children are not harmless. Girls, they are too numerous. Graceless children, mad with grief, they do not say amusing things or put their shoulders to the wheel, their noses to the grindstone; they do not link arms and present a touching wall against adversity. Useless, inconsolable, they are mean to their mother and to him and to each other. They have mysteriously lost their looks. They are unkempt, reckless in their speech and dress and attitude. He is powerless to help them. He looks at Elizabeth. Her face is red, as red as the face of any of his prone-to-weep innocent, desolate daughters. At once he says, "Don't. Don't do it, Lutz, don't cry." If you cry, Lutz,

---

he thinks, I will tell you. If he tells her, he will tell the world. If he speaks of it, he will never again speak of anything else. No one knows of Bud's wife's illness at the agency. No one but the sullen girl in Benefits, bribed in one way or another to keep quiet.

Elizabeth makes a tiny bleating sound. It reminds him of the bleat of the chemo machine. Every three weeks his wife has a five-day round of chemo in the hospital. He is in and out. He misses quite a lot of work that way. His wife fears the menacing chemo machine. Looking on its stanchion like a robot, like a traffic light. Bleating and squealing incoherent alarms. Self-important, a false savior. Bud's wife, Bud feels, needs to have Bud beside her. He leaps to his feet and slaps the apparatus sharply, shutting up its whining. He silences its senseless, ignominious complaints. He can make his wife laugh, even now.

Bud is forty-six and has overheard himself described as "one of the older guys." If he had a drug problem, a booze problem, they, the agency, might exercise a little fashionable latitude. But he is only a bit of a boozer, nothing showy. Sometimes he goes, at lunch, to the big, sordid Howard Johnson's near the agency and laps up cheap watery drinks. No one from the agency is likely to run into him. But he has seen Elizabeth Lutz there.

Beautiful Elizabeth, sobbing across the table from an older guy, a man worse dressed than Bud Heally. The man did not try to comfort Lutz, he said something sharp to her. And he left her there. And so did Bud Heally.

"Take another wallop at that Call Report," he says, "something along the lines of very productive session."

"Learning experience," Elizabeth says. "Definitely getting there. Clarified objectives. Enthusiastic concurrence. To what, though?"

"Long-term goals," he says.

She touches the inside of his wrist, where his pulse drums. He thinks he can hear her heart beating, but it must be the turning wheels of the Metroliner. "Do they call you Betty, I mean, did they? Or did they call you Liz?" A lot of pretty girls have worked for Bud Heally. His wife was pretty, is pretty, but these kids were pretty in another league. Once he fell in love with one. Another had a crush on him and then it went away. This thing with Elizabeth is, as they say, different. He takes Elizabeth's hand and begins to kiss her fingerbones. He has never before kissed a woman's hand; he wonders why. He sees that the awful nails are fake and probably expensive. He is vastly, secretly amused and touched by this. They are some kind of talisman. He thinks of his littlest girl, who wears a hat to bed and two hats should she rise to visit the bathroom. At the same time, he is hot with desire. He can have Elizabeth, whatever that means, have her. He kisses the bony fingers of her uglified young hand.

"In the eventuality that you leave your wife next week," Elizabeth Lutz says, "you know, hit her with the other shoe, should I hold myself in readiness?"

Ah, Lutz, he thinks, do that, do that. Hold yourself in readiness. But not for me. He is not required to say anything, because the train is pulling into the station.

167

The One
Without
the Parsley
Is the One
Without
the Poison

Doe's friend Ruby took the train to Belmont and brought back nearly seven hundred dollars and a man's new Burberry raincoat with cocaine in one of its pockets.

Ruben was carried away with himself and left Doe maybe twenty messages, most of them in unsuitable places.

Doe got off a little early for a change, which was good because she was really down. Doe is a caseworker for the city, responsible for a coven of dilapidated old people, some of them too clamorous, some of them too meek, all of them desperate for Doe's attention. What's more, her mother has died in Canada and she has had to make a quick trip up there to talk to people about the death. The people were the police, actually, and they hadn't been easy on her, or nice, although or because she hadn't seen her mother in, as the cops kept saying, "two to five *years*?"

Doe is wearing a pair of her dead mother's boots. Too small, though not by much, they are tight and shiny, too new, too flashy, too red and hopeful to discard or give away without disloyalty.

The boots hurt Doe terribly and make her think of the Little Mermaid, or possibly not the little one, some mermaid, who had her tail split so she could walk on earth and cohabit with mammalian males. Or, it being a fairy story, only one male, a prince at that. However it turned out, and Doe cannot remember, the mermaid's new feet hurt in a major way, which in Doe's experience takes the bloom off romance. And Ruby is not romance even, he is a semi-crony.

On the painful trek from her subway stop to her apartment building, Doe feels her odd, accustomed mixture of anticipatory pleasure and guilt. The building she lives in is so decent, the block it is on so "good"; her apartment, though tiny, is sunny and clean and expensive and almost, insofar as such a thing is possible, safe. Her mad old clients, on the other hand, live in danger and dirt, in basic rude debasing discomfort.

As expiation, tough little Doe has made her home the doily capital of the world. Crocheted artifacts and inept crafts of shoddy permanence crowd her. Some of these she inherited from the grandmother who raised her, complaining of it every faltering step of the way; some of them are gifts from fond or manipulative or merely timid clients.

169

They are all invested with an irritating sacredness before which Doe is helpless. She is also a pushover for farting relict bulldogs and three-legged pussies whose human former mommies have moved on to the pound in the sky. All of the animals are endlessly ailing or fasting or famished or moody, and it is in the search for free advice that she has run on Ruben, who runs a fancy though unprofitable pet shop in the neighborhood.

As she approaches her building's marquee this night, Hector, the prettiest of the doormen, dances out at her.

"Yo, Doughball," he cries with his usual glee, "you walk like you got a load in your panties, better you give them cowboy boots to me." He narrows his eyes. "Ruby told me," he recites: "Meet him at the horse joint."

"I don't want to meet Ruby at the horse joint," Doe says bitterly. "He wins a few bucks, he has to buy me dinner at the *horse joint?*"

"Is terrible," Hector says. "When I, personally, buy you the meal, it is not at the horse joint. What it is, the horse joint?"

Hector has trouble, adorable trouble, with his *j*'s. Doe wonders if he knows this. Hector is about nineteen. He has skin like an apricot and black dancing eyes. His hips are very narrow and his bum is very high. His mouth and nose are first-class work, his tumble of soft curly hair has a gloss like a child's. Doe considers telling him that her mother has died. His eyes will well with tears, he will embrace her and mouth around in a sympathetic way on her neck. She will get to smell his awful cologne, it is called ¡Señor!, close up, and his sweat.

But no. Hector will send her a huge, costly, appalling sympathy card and she will be obliged to keep it forever.

———

The One Without the Parsley Is the One Without the Poison

She considers describing the horse joint to Hector. It is the dismal upstairs restaurant area of an offtrack betting parlor. Ruby will make her eat his celebrational meal: smoked salmon, steak, chocolate mousse, bottle of Valpolicella. This meal sounds okay, but in Ruby's choice of restaurants it always tastes like airline food. But Ruby, to be fair, wouldn't know that, because Ruby never eats any anything. If Doe tells Hector some of this, he will cluck and mourn and coddle her. And then he will say, "What it is, dismal?"

"I walked all dogs for you," Hector says, instead. "Empty cat pee box, give parrot pill, lousy bugger, all took care of. You owe me one."

"Hector," Doe says, touched, since Hector knows she's a deadbeat when it comes to tips, never having two nickels left to rub together.

"Is okay, Miss Doughball," Hector says. "Ruby in bad trouble. Also I like to peek in you bureau draw, try on all you panty."

•　　•　　•

"You're walking like you're gut shot," Ruby says in the restaurant, where there is a ten-dollar minimum and a five-dollar entry fee or ten dollars if the man doesn't have his own jacket. The menu is printed on the paper place mat and is full of ampersands. Ruby insists Doe have the Irish Smoked Salmon Served with Capers, Onions & Tomato to be followed by New York Sirloin Steak (French Fries, Lettuce & Tomato). The crowd is mopey; horseplayers don't seem to run to animation.

"I'm going to handicap this race for you," Ruby says. He

scribbles on a sort of program that says "Yonkers" and "Bet with your head—not over it" and lists horses and jockeys and odds. The only thing about this leaflet that pleases Doe is some of the horses' names. Daddy's Money is nice and Most Beauty Girl. Most of it makes no sense to her: WPS D/D Ex Pace NW 4/or 25,000 LT C, H&G IM.

She knows Ruby would be, as he says, all too happy to explain these things, and also the big screen that displays the races, and the tote boards that keep changing and the newsreel-type band of electronic information that details the progress of some game somewhere, basketball, hockey. But she feels that her head is already full of things and the information Ruby imparts might shove out something interesting or useful.

On the other hand, she likes to listen to Ruby mutter horse talk. "The four with the one three five," Ruby mumbles, "I don't like the horse, I could be wrong. The G horse is not taking money. Twenty to one, the horse could win if twenty people carried it over the line. I'm gonna knock their little gizzard in. Little smashy noses. I hate the race, I don't like it. Gimme a B and GH."

Sometimes, during a race, Ruby, who seems not even to be watching, will yell, "He broke, get back in." Or "Attitude." Or "Come on, I bet the chalk."

Ruby would like Doe to place bets. Doe never places bets. "You'll go up to the window, you'll say what I say to say, you'll get a thrill."

"I don't want to get a thrill," Doe says, "I want to get some information. Why does Hector think you're in trouble? I thought you won a lot of money."

"Country girl, seven hundred dollars is not a lot of money."

"Seven hundred dollars is nice," Doe says. "You were happy about it, I thought."

"Oh, happy," Ruby says. And it is true, Ruby doesn't and hasn't and couldn't look happy. "Try this on," Ruby says. "It's a Burberry." He half raises from the chair beside him an enormous raincoat encrusted with tabs and loops, rings and epaulets, flappy attachments meant, it seems, to hold pikes and sabers, muzzle-loaders, rocket-launchers, hand grenades, and atom bombs.

"Douse that light, Soldier," Doe says.

"Sorry?"

"He was huge. You won this from the drug guy? Doing what? Putting the shot? Thumb wrestling? Remembering recording groups of the fifties? He was huge, Ruby."

"I'm sitting on the train," Ruby says, "sitting on the train, guy sits next to me, big guy. Him and his fucking raincoat is eating up the seat. I give him the look but not too much of the look because he's huge. He peels off the Burberry, he throws it on the seat, I think he's going to take the seat across from me, but, no, he catches something, some signal, some look, some sound. He charges out of there, leaves the threads behind him. I lay low, I fold it very casually over my arm, I debark. Later come to find out, guy left Bolivian crop dust in the pocket."

"Much?"

"Enough, what? Much? Too much if a cop picks me up. I bring it home. I'm thinking, Doe will kill for this."

"For Bolivian crop dust?"

"Shhhh," Ruby goes, sliding his eyes left and right. "Keep your voice down, act natural."

"Get used to it, Ruby, this is as natural as I know how to act. Is it a lot of dope?"

Ruby shakes the big raincoat and hefts it toward her. "Try it on."

Ruben's customers give him things and send him things: greeting cards, snaps of Pussikins and His Dogness, plaster, plastic, Baccarat crystal, lead, tin, papier-mâché, plush. They expect to see the cards and snaps and some of the stuffed toys in his shop, but they evidently mean the other goods for Ruby's private life. Ruby claims not to have a private life. He offloads on Doe. The result is one of the reasons Doe never asks anyone up to her apartment. Unable as she's been to turn down Ruby's innocent junk, she finds herself deeply unwilling to accept the awful raincoat. "Too big."

"Try it on."

"Too big. You keep it." This makes no sense, since Ruben is smaller than Doe.

"All your clothes don't fit you, now you draw the line?"

"My clothes are hand-me-downs from shrewder friends who went into public relations."

"Lose those boots, kid, take the raincoat."

The raincoat will live forever and she will take pity on it if she takes it at all. She will move through desolate neighborhoods wrapped in eccentric yards of high-cost affected imperialist British canvas, formerly the garb of some loathsome drug lord.

"The boots belonged to my mother."

"Ghoulish. Forget her. Don't think about her."

"I don't want to forget her. I don't want to think about her, either."

"She didn't do you no favors, Doe. Didn't even leave you a note."

"I consider that a favor. Also she didn't die from that.

———

174

She had another stroke, she always had them. Stroked out for once."

"That's not what the Mounties had to say."

"Wrong, wrong, you weren't there, I was. She'd been injecting herself with some stuff and injecting oranges and I think it was a melon, you know, but not to hurt herself. They told her at work at that cheesy storefront clinic she'd sunk to that she could no longer do injections. She was showing herself she could, I think. Or practicing. She used to be an anesthesiologist."

"Injecting herself with what, stove polish?"

"It was contact lens solution she was using, like saline or distilled water. Innocuous. Not drugs, not poison."

"They told you this?"

"They will, they will. I saw her place. There was an egg in a saucepan on the stove. She wouldn't put an egg on to boil and then say *adiós, amigos*."

"Why not?"

"Because. She got manicures. She had hair appointments. She read magazines about clothes. Loved clothes."

"So why were they taking her license away?"

"She was crazy. Couldn't treat a patient wearing green. Couldn't make notations in the charts, a bright light bouncing off them blinded her. Told people to sleep with their feet pointing toward the National Cathedral, something."

"My original mother probably lives in a trailer in a swamp," Ruby says. "On cinder blocks. No bottom teeth in her mouth. Bald."

"Pontoons in a swamp," Doe says. "Why bald?"

"The two things I inherited from her I hate—bad teeth and stupid hair."

"Well, you had them fixed," Doe says. Ruby's teeth have

been veneered with some nacreous substance. The dentist, if he was a dentist, recommended by one of Ruben's customers, eschewed painkillers but believed in aroma therapy and burning joss sticks. "Who did those teeth?" total strangers say to Ruby. "A priest of an Eastern order," Ruby says. After that Ruby's ordinary, thinning hair, hidden most of the time under a Greek captain's cap, was replenished or replaced, so that now a thick Prince Valiant–shaped helmet of black stuff rides on his skull. These alterations drained a lot of money from his business and have rendered him, in Doe's opinion, grotesque. He is a very small man; he told Doe once that he wanted to be a jockey but couldn't make the weight. He could make the weight now, he is thin and haggard; he coughs and rattles when he breathes.

"She had kids after me that were keepers," Ruby says. "She didn't have to give me up."

"Sure, she did," Doe says. She wonders if Ruby really knows anything about his mother and if he does, what it is, and how he found it out. And why. "Some social worker like me had her by the Peter Pan collar. She was what, thirteen? The thing used to be to talk up the middle-class couples dying for good babies; opportunities you couldn't hope to offer the kid yourself. Think of your future, get on with your life, let the healing begin. Like that."

"So maybe she was just some tart."

"For just some tart, the same line of chat, believe me."

"Still," Ruby says. "Will you inherit any gelt from your mother?"

"My mother was geltless. Whatever she had, not much, will go in some lawsuit. She fucked somebody up. Also,

176

I'm not lending you a cent again, ever. No hard feelings."

"I was wishing you'd have a nut to pay your vet bills."

"What vet bills? Unless somebody needs a hemorrhoidectomy, you're my vet."

"I'm history," Ruby says. "The poodle parlor's history. They shut me down."

"I didn't know that."

"No kidding," Ruby says with heavy irony. "I somehow figured that it made the papers."

"Well, you didn't pay much attention to it, Ruben. You didn't run it very well. I don't even know if you enjoyed it."

"Shut up, Doe."

"Can't one of the rich ladies help you? The ones you walk? The ones you escort to the opera when their hairdressers are busy?"

"They did that already. In the last location. It gets old."

Doe herself has been dispatched to a chic address by Ruby. A cared-for blond woman with a surgical stare, described by Ruby as one of the top society babes, took her silently into the kitchen of a very grand apartment. The woman reached into the freezer, withdrew an aluminum-foil packet, put it in Doe's hands, and whispered, "Nine hundred dollars." For the moment Doe feared that she had just bought some contraband that cost nine hundred dollars when all she had was the taxi fare that Ruben had given her, and that was, in fact, the condition on which she'd run this peculiar errand. But the woman peeled back a corner of the foil for Doe and there, cold and a little damp: nine hundred dollars.

It was a furtive transaction, redolent of blackmail or something equally seedy, but perhaps it was inspired by friendly feeling, or customer satisfaction. Or pity.

"I don't have any money to give you, Ruby."

"Money, I spit on it. I want to give you my fish."

"Fish," Doe says, and the certainty of doom floods over her. "Not fish."

"Fish. I saved out some cases of cat food and dog food. Parrot food I never carried, that lousy bugger is on his own."

"Ruby, not fish."

"Fish," Ruby says. "They turned off my juice. I couldn't get it up for the bill, which is like the population of a small republic, so this vindictive light company cut my juice. Somebody should stamp on their fingers, I swear to God. Here's fish without juice, no bubblers." He does a thing with his mouthful of teeth that is purely fish and funny and alarming. "Poor buggers. Wet *dogs* I've got, one big hairy beast about half clipped. Wet dogs: It's wet, it's dark, no blow in the blow-dryers, everybody cold and wet and hairy, sore as boils. Wet dog groomers, madder than the dogs." Ruby shakes himself, doing dogs, wet dogs, and laughing so hard, he is nearly helpless and horseplayers scowl at them from surrounding tables.

"Gary has a coffee enema appointment, no time to dry this doglet with a towel, if he could find a towel. Can't blow it out fluffy, no fluffy, no tip. Sophie is pregnant, everything hits on her hormones. Luther, you don't want to know."

"Couldn't you apply the seven hundred on the light bill? It's a little something, it's good faith."

"Good faith we have left in the dust," Ruby says. "It's light, it's telephone, the lease, a little spot of bother with, like, sales tax."

———

"Ruby, let's sell the raincoat guy's cocaine."

"You astonish me," Ruby says. He looks astonished, and frightened. "Keep your voice down, you baby in the woods, you. Forget it. Dismiss it from your tiny mind."

"How much could we get?"

"I'm feeling angry now. This is disturbing my peace of mind. This is not the person I know."

"It's not the person I know, either, but I want you to tell me how much we could get. We'll only sell it to already bad people. No fathers of families, no nursing mothers, no school-yard stuff."

"Tomorrow, Hector and me will install the tanks. You know nothing about it. You get home from work, it's fate accomplished, as they say in French. You're lucky I sold the snake. There's a gecko, but how much trouble is a gecko?"

"I'm a little bit put out by your high moral tone. I thought you were mad, bad, and dangerous to know."

"At this minute those tanks are like parked on a side street in an unmarked van, so to speak. They need a place to go."

"Take them to your place."

"Remember me, the guy who lives over the shop? I don't have a place."

"Why won't you tell me what the coke is worth?"

"Oh, to hell," Ruby says. "I'll flush the goddamn fish down the commode. The stuff, it isn't worth anything, it's a pinch, it's a pinch minus. You were expecting two kilos?"

"You made it sound like more."

"Give you a thrill."

"If it was more, would you sell it?"

"Yeah, sure. Maybe. Probably not. I did time, I don't want to get locked up for anything."

————

Moses Supposes

"Am I to understand you are a convicted drug dealer?"

"Convicted water dealer," Ruby says. "Ruben's No Guff Spring Water. Plain jug. It says on the label, 'The One Without the Parsley Is the One Without the Poison.' Classical allusion, like from the Marx Brothers, I think it was, or Danny Kaye. This is not spring water for ignorant jerks."

"So that's illegal?"

"As a matter of record, it came out of the tap. We ran it through filters, we blued it a little."

"That's crooked, but it doesn't sound like jail time."

"Very filthy filters evidently," Ruby says in a distant way, as though you couldn't prove it by him. "E. coli like you wouldn't wish it on your worst enemy."

"You're not really sick, are you?" Doe is contrite. She has, as is her custom, eaten his dinner as a chaser to her own. She examines him, a thing she seldom does. He is not a comfortable person on which to rest the eyes, always covered, as now, with shining snips of dog hair, never looking showered or properly shaved. Wigged and freshly supplied with luminous toothiness like a wolf in the woods, like a gigolo, a shark. He is translucently pale, frail as an ailing child. She is suddenly convinced that Ruben, unwashed, unlovely, unloved, and frighteningly mortal, is her charge.

"It's okay about the fish," she says with deep resentment. "It's not okay, but I'll do it for now." Ruben is going to die.

"Take the raincoat," Ruby says.

"You are intransigent."

"It's a Burberry."

"I'll only take it if you give me the stuff that was in the

pocket," Doe says sternly. She feels very strongly about this.

Ruby looks like an old, old, withered street creature. Ruben is going to die.

"Enjoy," he says. He hands over the enormous raincoat with its illicit invisible cargo. "Not here, though," he says, as though she were an uncontrollable cokehead. He is disappointed in her. But, she can see, he is tired.

•   •   •

The next day, Doe takes the raincoat with her into one of the dirty toilet stalls in one of the dirty women's bathrooms in the unrelievedly dirty building the city devotes to social services. She looks in the raincoat's pockets. She expects to find what they call "a glassine envelope" in police reports. She expects this to look like the envelopes her stamps, when she collected stamps, came in. In memory they are all Moroccan stamps, red ones, with pictures of FDR on them, God knows why. But the envelope, when she finds it, is more like a tiny Ziploc bag. White powder, not very much of it, lurks inside this husk, shining a little, dangerous, unknown. Of course, it might be talcum or cornstarch or ground-up Tums. Doe hates and fears drugs and feels guilty swallowing an aspirin. She has only lately begun to drink wine, hitherto fearing that her brain, confronted with the mildest insult, would bleed, as her mother's had since Doe's birth. One of her old clients saved her out a marijuana cigarette from a supply bestowed by a compassionate doctor to help with his cancer pain. The client said he understood young people—all Doe's clients

181

regard her as a young person—enjoyed such things. She still has it. Another client has given her a jar full of Elavil, which the client evidently feels are tonic but too modern for her, like vitamins or kelp or blue-green algae. Doe has those. All she knows about the ingestion of cocaine she has learned from advertisements purporting to discourage its use. She has brought with her a pocket mirror, a razor blade; she has rolled up a new dollar bill.

She considers the hundreds of case histories she has read, the ingenious atrocities, for example, perpetrated upon children by parents who used merely to beat them or roast their fingers in gas flames. Atrocities attributed to the use of powder like this. Still, the little rind of stuff has a potent attraction. It is rebel powder, it is power of a sort. Its use will indicate to her that she is not yet entirely the person she knows herself to be. But even as she thinks these things, she feels the weight of her own nature on her back, heavy as a monkey, familiar as a Jones. She will go home today to bubbling walls of lighted fish. Some tomorrow soon she will go home to Ruby, Ruby or someone like Ruby. No, face it, Ruby. She will make him a bed on the floor, in a corner. Eventually, she will give him her own bed and she will sleep on the floor, wrapped in the raincoat, heavy as her knowledge of her character, too heavy for comfort but not, apparently, too heavy to bear.

She will lose sleep to bubblers, to tiny luminous castles, gleaming fish. Visited by cold, damp noses in the night, lulled by swooning purrs. Cursed by parrots, anchored to reality by fleas. Ruby will cough and die. But not rapidly. Doe's feet will hurt.

Doe throws the envelope into the toilet and tries to flush

it down. Water laps out and wets her foot. She succeeds in flushing the toilet at last and three or four other toilets, so inept is the plumbing, flush in concert. "Observe the fugues coming in," Doe thinks.

She leaves the raincoat in the stall, but of course there is no escaping it. It is back at her desk before she is. Waiting for her.

Whatever
You Say,
Say Nothing

And what was the first thing her husband said to her, after the birth of their child, as she lay reverent, chastened, smug, and remarkably uncomfortable, owing to thirty-two stitches?

"I fully expected you to die," he said, in the pally tone he used for such confidences. "So I could go off with Andy and live happily ever after."

"Andy" she assumed to be a diminutive of Andrea, although, on the other hand, God knew. She looked at the ceiling track along which curtains around her bed ineffectively traveled. She looked across the room at the two Italian girls. They were cousins, eighteen and nineteen years old. They had labored briefly and noisily and been re-warded with robust infants and veal-and-pepper sub-marines. They had hot-eyed, whispering husbands, one already a little bald, one so hairy as to be almost fur-bear-ing. Neither of these nice young men appeared to have her own husband's unappeasable appetite for disapproval. "All right, Malachy," she said, "I didn't die. So what's plan B?"

"I've looked at the child," Malachy said, "and I'm sure it's a very nice child, but I just don't feel anything for it."

"As I understand it," she said, "it's sort of a blind date. You gradually grow on each other. Or else, of course, you don't."

"These are terrible things to say to you," Malachy said.

"Not at all," she said, although she quite agreed. "Just spit it out in Mommy's hand."

"I suppose you'll want a divorce," he said.

"Who, me? Not me. It's years since I wanted a divorce."

Malachy hung around awhile, hoping for a few cruel words, and then he went away.

$\bullet \quad \bullet \quad \bullet$

Her mother came to see her. Her mother was the sexiest person she knew, in the sense that a militant atheist may be said to be religious. She was also loving and baffled and cranky. Her mother prodded and tugged at her gown and her bedclothes. In the interests of a greater decency, but also, Baby knew—for she was called Baby and always had been—for the pleasure of touching her.

"That's a little more Protestant-looking," Baby's mother said, scowling. She sat down, well out of reach, and crossed her ankles. "It's a beautiful child, God love it," she said without ardor.

"I know it," Baby said. "I feel exalted. I feel like Tisket when she's just hatched out another batch of kittens. Did you feel that way, Ma?"

"Tisket's near had her eye tore out by some filthy ruffin of a tom. That orange ruffin with the spots. All he needs is a cap and a pipe and a muffler and he'd be the image of your Daddy."

"Oh, God," Baby said. "But we are agreed that it is a beautiful child."

"It is. But. You'd want to hear how his people are getting on about it. It's got Malachy's eyes and Malachy's nose and Malachy's mouth. They've left us nothing but the ears."

"That child doesn't look a thing in the world like Malachy," Baby said.

"Why wouldn't it?" her mother said, with her air of justified foreboding. "A child looks like its father and Malachy is his father. The child looks just like Malachy and we'll say no more about it."

"Ma," Baby said.

"I'm sure you think it's very clever to suggest things like that, but I don't think it's clever and I don't think it's nice."

"I'm not suggesting, you're suggesting. I don't look all that much like Daddy, in brute fact."

"If you have an accusation to bring against me," Baby's mother said, dappled, seeping tears, "I'd be glad if you'd bring it in plain words."

"Ma, whatever I did or whatever I said, I'm sorry I did it or said it."

"I'm tired of the sound of that," Baby's mother said. She

blotted her blunt, soft kitten face with a wad of flowered tissues.

"So am I," Baby said. She looked across at the Italian girls. Various handsome women, no older than Baby's older sisters, batted around over there, doing chirpy, cozy things. "Well, back to the brighter side," she said. "I'm glad the kid is up to snuff."

"Oh, the kid," Baby's mother said. "You bring forth a child, you bring forth sorrow. Molly was my first and you were my last and I had five others in between and every single one of you was aggravation and sorrow."

"Well, I was there," Baby said, "and that's not the way I remember it."

"Nobody was there but me," Baby's mother said. "Molly's got cancer."

"I know that."

"In her mouth."

"I know. Who told you?"

"Nobody *told* me," Baby's mother said.

"Molly's handling it awfully well," Baby said. By this she meant that Molly was informed, amused, and anecdotal to a truly appalling degree.

"Well, I'm not," Baby's mother said.

"Not me either," Baby said. "I know how you feel."

"You don't know anything," her mother said. She stood up and buttoned her coat. It was almost impossible to get Baby's mother dislodged from Baby's mother's coat except inside her own house. "It's a lovely child," she said. "I just hope you take care of it."

"I was planning to neglect it."

"Well, don't." She walked toward the door. But there she

---

hesitated and returned. "I want to tell you just one thing I'm sure of," she said, in a musing, almost tender, way.

"Tell me," Baby said. "Tell me. What?"

"It's about time you pulled up your socks," Baby's mother said, and so saying, departed.

·   ·   ·

"Would you like to compare obstetrical notes?" Baby asked Andrea, when Andrea appeared with her crocheting.

"No. No," Andrea said.

"Did you see the baby?"

"Yes," Andrea said.

"Well?"

"Well," Andrea said, in apparent commiseration, "you know most of them don't look like much right away. They shape up, though."

"I thought he looked pretty good, myself," Baby said. "Did you think he resembled Malachy?"

"I don't know," Andrea said. "Shouldn't he? The six-year-old is writing upside down. The youngest one's ear is infected again. I think the nine-year-old is shooting dope."

The nine-year-old, the six-year-old, and the youngest one were Andrea's children. At first Baby had thought that Andrea disliked these three about whom she endlessly fretted and complained. But soon she realized that, so passionate was Andrea's feeling for her tiresome, charming, ordinary children, she feared to speak their names.

"Well?" Andrea said.

" 'Well' what?"

"I said I think the nine-year-old is shooting dope."

———

"Unlikely," Baby said.

"Sniffing it," Andrea said. "Smoking it?"

"Nope. Possibly."

"What do you mean, *possibly?*" Andrea said. "The child is nine years old."

"Kids these days," Baby said.

"What do you know about kids these days?"

"I know their mothers suspect them of shooting dope when they're only nine years old," Baby said. "I know I just had a baby," Baby said. "I know my best friend is sleeping with my husband."

"Oh, that," Andrea said, greatly relieved.

"That."

"Didn't amount to a hill of beans," Andrea said. "Whatever that amounts to. Where did that expression originate? All he did was hold my handlebars."

"Don't tell me," Baby said.

"Suits me."

"I guess you'd better tell me."

"We went biking in the park now and then," Andrea said. "I thought I was getting too chummy with my children."

"And how did you do this without my knowing?"

"Well, we lied," Andrea said. "It's the only efficient way, really."

"You don't even like men," Baby said. "All you care about is those dreary children."

"Well, that's true," Andrea said, displeased. "But I draw the scorn and contempt crowd. And speaking of dreary, do you know what the nurses call little Malachy-Malachy-Jr.-Jr. in the nursery? They call him Rubber Ducky. Because he squawks *all the time*. Speaking of dreary."

———

"And so now you and Malachy want to get married."
"Well, I didn't," Andrea said, "but maybe now I do."

•   •   •

"If we'd really wanted an infant," Malachy said broodily, "we could have adopted a little black one."
"Golly," Baby said. "Why didn't I think of that?"

•   •   •

Baby's father came to visit her, bringing with him her brother Leo, the second eldest of his children. Leo was a foreman in a paper box factory. He worked a lot of overtime. Leo drove an Eldorado and wore custom-made cowboy boots. He lived in the cellar of his parents' house. He raised Kerry Blue terriers. He said very little, but whatever he said, he said three times. (They called him Ditto at the box factory.) He gave away, to his brother, his sisters, his parents, his nephews and nieces, the Redemptorist Purgatorial Society, and the Maryknoll Missions, all the money he didn't need for his Eldorado and his cowboy boots and his Kerry Blues. Every once in a while her father and Leo went off together on a prolonged and dangerous drunk. These terrified the family. Masses, rosaries, and other, less pious things were said. However, the only accepted idiom for these ghastly episodes was "toot," as in "Daddy and Leo have gotten a snootful and gone on a toot." She assumed that her father paid for the snootfuls on the toots. Once in a while Leo had shock treatments and she knew her father paid for those.

"This is a great day, Baby," her father said resentfully.

———

He grabbed her by the shoulder and kissed her on the mouth. He always kissed his daughters on the mouth when he particularly disapproved of them. Baby considered that her mother, as was her practice, was right. Her father did look like a little old spotted orange tomcat. Leo looked like Central Casting's idea of a pope.

"Kiss her, Leo."

"Leo doesn't want to kiss me."

"Leo wants to lend you his police-band radio."

Leo had a bundle in his arms, wrapped in a fragment of blanket. He held it lovingly, stroking it from time to time.

"Leo doesn't have to do that," Baby said. "Lend me his radio."

"Leo *wants* to do that," her father said. "Do you *mind?*"

"Daddy," Baby said.

"It's the mother that turned you against Leo," her father said. "Leo never raised his hand to you."

"Good Lord," Baby said. "I should hope not."

"Leo's got more good in him than the rest of you added together," her father said. "It was the mother that was the ruin of Leo. But don't you come over that to her, now."

"Okay," Baby said. "Did you and Leo see the grandson?"

"Maybe we did and maybe we didn't. I can't tell the one from the other and never could. Couldn't pick my own squad out of the tribes on the streets. Couldn't tell Molly and Teresa from Catherine and Joan."

"Catherine has red hair," Baby said helpfully.

"Catherine had red hair and you were wall-eyed," he said. "And still I couldn't tell the one of you from the next one."

"That's very interesting," Baby said. "I never noticed that."

191

"You never noticed nothing," her father said bitterly. "None of you never noticed nothing. Where's the big fellow?"

"Malachy's not so big. He's nowhere near as big as Leo."

"It would do him the world of good if he'd remember that."

Leo spoke. "Hold on. Hold on. Hold on," Leo said. These remarks were addressed to himself. His voice was low and urgent.

"Why are you sore at me?" Baby asked her father.

"Don't be talking," her father said. "Don't be talking."

"You have at least twenty-eight grandchildren," Baby said. "So I made it twenty-nine. So you and Leo get a case of the huffs, and the next thing I know you'll have wrecked some gin mill."

"There's no harm in Leo," her father said. "No harm at all. But somebody'd better cast an eye to his welfare once I shuffle off. I had it in mind that it might be you. But *you* had it in mind that it mightn't be."

"Oh, God," Baby said. "In the first place . . . I don't know what's in the first place. But that is flat-out loony."

"Hold on," Leo said. "Hold on. HOLD ON."

"In the first place," Baby said, when she was sure that Leo had finished, "you're going to live forever."

"Six to eight months," the old man said triumphantly. "Heart, lungs, liver, legs. Circulation's almost gone in the legs. Maybe a year. It's possible that I could last a year."

"I'm pretty sure I don't believe you," Baby said.

"Time will tell," her father said in a chipper way that was almost more than she could stand. "In the meantime, say nothing to your mother. Whatever you say, say nothing. Leo," he said. "Tell Magdalene what you came to tell her."

Leo deposited the swaddled radio gently on the bed. He took two new folded fifty-dollar bills from his watch pocket and fitted them into her palm and closed her fingers over them. "One of these days," he said. "One of these days. One of these days." For a moment she saw Leo as the Italian girls might be seeing him. He was heroic in scale and very handsome, in the way that was sometimes called "distinguished." He said very little, but what he said seemed to mean something, at least to him.

"One of these days, Leo," Baby said. But Leo looked frightened, and she stopped.

·   ·   ·

"I certainly hope you people know what you're doing," Malachy's mother said. Malachy's mother was a pretty woman, chronically doubtful.

"I certainly hope so," said Baby.

"I hope that child is, you know, right," Malachy's mother said. "I read an article. I was going to bring it and then I said to myself, 'Don't bring it, it might affect her milk.' How is your milk?"

"Fine," Baby said. "Very nice."

"The worst thing about having a baby is it makes your bosom floppy."

"I sincerely hope," Baby said, "that's the worst thing."

"Cocoa butter," Malachy's mother said. "Barbells."

"Thank you."

"Thirty-two stitches," Malachy's mother said. "Malachy said to me, 'Mother, Baby had thirty-two stitches,' and I said to him, 'Malachy, that means just one thing to me. Baby must have very lazy muscles in her birth canal.'"

•   •   •

"It was really nice of you to come," Baby said to her brother Jacky-the-priest.

"Oh, hell," Jacky-the-priest said, "I always liked you." He was wearing Earth Shoes. He was pink and plummy. His belly lapped over his belt. She remembered him as a tall, pale, beautiful boy who loved only his mother and basketball and God.

There'd been murmurs of a brilliant gift, a grand career; he'd spent a little time in Rome. But somewhere, somehow, it had all, without any known drama, gone askew. Now he was an assistant pastor in a small parish in Connecticut. His fatness and pinkness seemed unconnected with any appetite. He was sad and cheery. His family and he no longer intimidated each other.

"How's Fodder?" Baby said. Fodder was Father Clancy, his pastor.

"Like always," Jacky said. "Pissing and moaning. He made me give away my little dog."

"He can't do that."

"That's where you're mistaken."

"Ma gave you that dog," Baby said. "You love that dog."

"Leo took it back," Jacky said. "I visit it every chance I get. I didn't really come to see you—I came to see my dog. I'm just working you in." He laughed. His eyes were swimming.

———

194

"Oh, God, Jacky," Baby said. "I should never have had this child."

"It'll be all right," Jacky said. "Ma doesn't even know the dog is back. She can't tell one dog from another."

"Daddy can't tell one *child* from another."

"Daddy doesn't know it's back, either," Jacky said. "Only Leo. Thank God for Leo."

"One day," Baby said, "Leo is going to pick up a box-making tool and cleave some citizen from his crown to his crotch."

"You may be right," Jacky said. "The really awful thing is that I frankly couldn't give a shit. Because I know that Leo will never be mean to my dog."

"Leo's little nephew is down the hall in the nursery," Baby said.

"He'll be all right," Jacky-the-priest said. "Leo's all right. There's no harm in Leo."

"Is that the most I can ask for my child?" Baby said. "That he should be harmless?"

"It's not the worst he could be," Jacky said. "Catherine's kid's not harmless. Teresa's kid's not harmless. Joan's kid's not harmless. Two of those kids set the other kid up for a fall."

"I don't believe that," Baby said. "They're not bad kids."

"Of course not, they're just kids who do bad things."

"You wouldn't believe the bad things I've done, Jacky," Baby said. "Or rather, I guess you would."

"Oh, sure," Jacky said. He seemed bored.

"Of course, as far as you're concerned I'm not even a married woman," Baby said.

"Oh, sure," Jacky said. "You'll be all right. What I keep thinking is, that's a pretty nice cellar Leo has there. Rug on the floor, table and chairs. It's clean, it's dry. Just the freezer and the oil burner and an apple box full of nice little puppies."

"You used to talk a lot about *agape* and *eros* and things like that," Baby said. "You haven't done much of that lately."

"Not lately," Jacky said.

"Aren't you even going to give me your blessing?" Baby said.

"I'll give you mine if you'll give me yours," he said. He put his hand on her head and said the words. And then to her astonishment he knelt before her and waited. She put her hand in his hair and rubbed it, mumbling. His hair felt alien. She hadn't touched Jacky in years.

On his way out he stopped dutifully at the beds of the two Italian girls for, as it were, pastoral calls.

•　　•　　•

"I wish we could be like other people," Malachy said. "But I don't think we can."

"Nobody's like other people," Baby said. "Other people aren't like other people."

"We should have discussed this thing more thoroughly," Malachy said. "We shouldn't have rushed headlong into it."

"Malachy," Baby said. "Oh, Malachy."

•　　•　　•

Molly, Baby's sister, came. Her speech was badly slurred. She was thin and luminous. "I want to tell you about your godchild," Molly said.

"She isn't my godchild, really," Baby said with caution. "Not technically."

"She is in the eyes of God," Molly said.

"Terrific," Baby said. "The God's-eye view."

"When Maggie was learning to talk and I couldn't make out what she was babbling," Molly said, "I used to tease her, I used to say, 'I'm sure you're right.' And now she speaks so beautifully and she can't understand me, not a word. And do you know what that little mischief says to me?"

" 'I'm sure you're right,' " Baby said.

" 'I'm sure you're right,' " Molly said. "Isn't that the funniest? 'I'm sure you're right.' "

• • •

Baby's elegant sister Catherine came. Her beautiful red hair was tatty and unwashed. Every few minutes her eyes squeezed shut and she flinched in a tic. "I just can't bring myself to care what happens to that kid," she said. "He's a rotten kid. The other kids are good kids, but that one is trouble."

"He's your favorite," Baby said.

"Of course he's my favorite," Catherine said. "What have I got, good sense? Naturally he's my favorite."

• • •

Baby's sister Teresa came. She was growing squat and veiny and having trouble with what she called her pressure. "Still and all," she said to Baby, "kids are the best thing that ever happened to me."

"That's really nice to hear," Baby said.

"On the other hand," Teresa said, for Teresa was vigorously truthful, "kids are the *only* thing that ever happened to me."

• • •

When Baby's sister Joan found her, she was shuffling around in the solarium, a dank and sunless room. "You missed all the excitement," Joan said.

"One of the Italian girls is dead," Baby said. "Both of them maybe."

"Greek. They're Greek. She isn't dead. She has a Teflon valve in her heart and they give her this medication to thin her blood and keep her valve from clogging. And what do you know, she's been bleeding from the kidneys."

"What do you know," Baby said.

"She's the one with the baby with the birthmark," Joan said, full of the exhilaration of crisis.

"There is no baby with a birthmark."

"Don't be ridiculous, of course there is. You couldn't miss that baby, she has a great big splashy port-wine stain all over the side of her face and head. Right over the eyelid and everything. It's a girl, too."

"There is no baby with a birthmark," Baby screamed, and Joan, rather pleased, bustled off to seek medical assistance.

• • •

"Is your name really Magdalene?" Olaf said. "I find that very amusing." He stroked the inside of her wrist with two fingers.

"It's a thigh-slapper, all right," Baby said. "Why don't you beat it on out of here?"

"I am a doctor," Olaf said weightily. "I wear a white coat. I have assumed protective coloration." In truth, he was a dentist, her dentist, and she had a comprehensive knowledge of his gastric rumbles that predated anything else in their relation. There were months when Olaf had provided comfort and delight, but comfort and delight had fled now, and the carcass of Olaf was left behind, stranded.

"I saw the child," Olaf said. "Do you think you will become attached to it?"

"I wouldn't be surprised," Baby said.

"And your husband? What of him? He is proud? Pleased? Delighted?"

"Oh, all of the above," Baby said, eager to be rid of Olaf, and alone, alone, alone, with her child. "Of course, being Malachy, he shows it in some very subtle ways."

Malachy had moved in with a dancer. A knobby, weepy boy named Andy, who brought the baby unsuitable toys. Malachy was gloomily in love, except when he was gloomily out of it. Nevertheless, he had warned his wife to regard all his arrangements as purely temporary. He said that he had to tread carefully. He said that Andy looked upon him as a father figure.

On the
Mountain
Stands
a Lady

Until the year that I met Mrs. Kevin-Spending, the obligation to grow into a woman lay light on me. Nothing else did, though. I spent that winter bivouacked at my cousin Teddy's house, dayhopping with her to her school, Dowd Academy. My father was dead and my mother was living in a hotel in Philadelphia. My cousin Teddy, whose bedroom I shared, prayed every night that I wouldn't be there in the morning. I prayed, too, but neither of us had any luck at it.

Teddy was beautiful beyond the sophomore class's sternest need, and organized. She won accolades on the hockey field. I, benched in some distant outskirt, feigned earache or a terrible cold. She was chosen to be Phaedra on Parents' Day. I lurked at the bottom of our French class, my mind a damp stain spreading to my mother, who had a job painting mottoes on ashtrays and propelled toward matrimony a rich and cagey florist.

I despised Dowd Academy. My old school, the Villa Maria, had been life as I had led it since my father died. Dowd Academy, in its ominous way, began to be life.

. . .

The evenings back at Teddy's house were no improvement, since every night a boy named Douglas Lambert came to call. Teddy took him out on the sun porch, to the record player and *The Prophet*. I sat in the living room, brooding, listening to my chubby aunt Electra, a talkative enthusiast of potted plants. Outside the window, in a golden cone of light, was high reality. From under a string of varnished gourds shone Dougie's profile, fierce against the cushion of the glider. My cousin Teddy was beside him, breasty and brainy and smug as a cat. Her hair was the color of marmalade.

Then a new French teacher came to Dowd Academy. She was Mrs. Kevin-Spending. I knew her at once as an emissary from the wide, illuminated world.

Mrs. Kevin-Spending had water-green eyes and a breathy, wicked voice. She appeared to be alight with a mild, pleasurable fever. From the tags of information that she flung at us like coins, it was easy to determine that her clothes had come from Paris. Her husband was a cousin of the Queen.

As soon as Mrs. Kevin-Spending entered a classroom,

she pulled down the shades. She was something to see in that artificial twilight. Sometimes she was antic, sometimes she was calm. Sometimes, between the Vowel Chart and the framed Procedure for Fire Drill, she was beset by a peculiar urgency, as though delivering a message in a complicated code. Where Miss Fogarty had merely made it clear that you would never learn French, Mrs. Kevin-Spending fluffed her gamine-cut, violet-washed hair, checked the moorings of a few of the things that floated or dangled from her, and added, relevantly, or with a merry, vagrant malice, that you were too tall, too short, too fat, too thin, pimpled, plain, much too smart or far from smart enough.

Dowd Academy was dazzled but doubtful. I was full of reverence. Mrs. Kevin-Spending was gorgeous, was hope. Her abundance and disorder caught me, and I saw in them the vistas of grown-upness. Not the measly local product, but a rich estate where people spoke French without trying, had never heard of hockey, where there were sun porches for all.

One day in class Mrs. Kevin-Spending told Teddy that she had *le regard de Venus*—a reference to Teddy's gilt-rayed, slightly mismatched eyes. Afterward she confronted us in the library, scribbled her address on a call slip, and told us to come and see her that evening. She said to bring our French books. I was overcome.

• • •

The lobby of Mrs. Kevin-Spending's apartment building was Moorish and spooky, dimly lighted by yellow lanterns and hung with oval mirrors of a wild and desolate blue. It smelled like a tunnel. We started upstairs. We passed a stained-glass window that opened on an air shaft and a black arrow, stenciled importantly on the wall, captioned DENTIST. Mrs. Kevin-Spending's door, unlabeled, was next to one marked CLEMENT FRISCHWASSER DDS RING BELL WALK IN.

Teddy knocked. Mrs. Kevin-Spending instantly opened the door, stepped outside, and closed it. Her velvet pajamas were a nervy shade of green, and she was spangled and spattered with mirror chips, but she didn't look glad to see us. Teddy handed her a rose. She took it, smiled deafly, and slipped a hand inside her bodice to finger after a lost shoulder strap. Then she pushed open the door, waving us over the threshold.

"Don't step on the rug," she said.

Teddy stopped short and the procession piled up, especially me.

"That," Mrs. Kevin-Spending said. She pointed to a scrap of figured carpet that lay inside the door. "Step over it, can't you, it's not for walking on."

We made our way through a hall and into a room overfull of black oak furniture, including a piano and a big bed. The bed was canopied in tired pink taffeta and looked, like everything else in the room, forlorn, as though it had been left over at the end of an auction. I was beginning to feel bad.

"Sit down," Mrs. Kevin-Spending said peevishly. "Don't mill around. Young people mill around so. It makes my nerves shoot out."

Teddy sat down on the outermost edge of a boudoir chair. Mrs. Kevin-Spending tilted a lamp so that it bathed her in a vicious glare.

———

"Sit, Isolde," she said to me, "sit, sit. You never do a thing you're told and that's your entire trouble."

I looked around for something to sit on. Chairs were ranged against the walls, but things were on them and under them. I was paralyzed. What bothered me most was the faint impropriety of being unexpectedly entertained in a room with a bed in it. Mrs. Kevin-Spending was watching me. I cleared off one of the chairs and lugged it out to the island of space near the bed. She hooked another lamp into a swarm of extension cords. It came suddenly abloom and shone full on her, and the paint around her eyes and on her mouth looked, for an instant, like a second, makeshift face scrawled teasingly across the first. It gave me the creeps. She set the lamp down beside me.

"Is that enough light on the subject?"

We assured her that it was. She began to circle me, gathering up art objects and relocating them out of elbow range. I didn't blame her, but I wished I could get her, in my mind's eye, back to her own, her original face.

Suddenly Teddy took a breath. "Do you *live* here?" she said, appalling me.

"What an unearthly question," Mrs. Kevin-Spending said, stopped in her tracks. "Of course I live here. Where would I live if I didn't live here?"

"Well, *I* don't know," Teddy said. "Miss Lieblich and Miss Fogarty used to have an apartment, but on weekends they went home or somewhere, so Miss Lieblich and Miss Fogarty really lived in houses."

"Did they?" Mrs. Kevin-Spending said. "Well, the Eskimos live in igloos and the Boy Scouts live in tents, but what that means to me I just don't know." She looked us over and sat down on the foot of the bed.

———

She smiled at us and we smiled back. The assembly took on an unpremeditated and provisional tone, as though it had evolved by accident, maybe in a slowly down-going elevator. After a while Mrs. Kevin-Spending fished a tangle of knitting from under a cushion. "Did I knit or did I purl?" she said, holding it aloft. "I purled." She worked several rows in silence. Teddy, who has never cared for the company of people who aren't making some kind of noise, sneezed nervously. I unfolded my hands and hung them down the sides of my chair, to dry. *Principes de Grammaire et de Style* went coasting off my lap. I very casually rested my foot on it.

"I was wondering what we were going to do tonight," I said, driven.

Mrs. Kevin-Spending stopped knitting. "We're going to sit quietly and express ourselves in short declarative sentences." She began knitting again.

"French sentences?" I said finally.

Mrs. Kevin-Spending gave me a look. A short look, but it was meaty. Vanquished, I stared at my saddle-shoed feet. My left foot was a whole size larger than my right foot, and even my right foot seemed quite a bit larger than it strictly needed to be.

"I was never like that," Mrs. Kevin-Spending said fastidiously. "I was as much like Thérèse as I was like anyone. Though, of course, I wasn't blond. Blond hair is unfortunate in the long view. It has a way of getting dismal."

Teddy crossed her eyes at Mrs. Kevin-Spending. I disapproved, but it was so precise that a little thud of joy moved between my collarbones. "I guess we're waiting for somebody," Teddy said on half a yawn. "I mean, are we or what?"

"We're waiting for Heather Lowenstein, who snuffs," Mrs. Kevin-Spending said ill-naturedly. She gave an illustrative snuff, not at all in Heather's manner. "And your friend with the sunlamp. *Ingrid*. Late to class every single session, but that's all right. She'll have a hide like an elephant before she's thirty." She pulled at a thread of beading at her cuff, breaking it and catching the glass beads in her palm. "We're waiting for that red-haired girl with the coat with the fur buttons," she said bitterly. "She's a very *sweet* girl, but she's got warts on her hands." She looked anxiously at her own hands, wartless. "I'm trying to give you certain advantages. You'll admit that Dowd is rather bare of advantages?"

I was ready to admit it. Teddy wasn't. "You have some beautiful pieces," she said calmly. "I can see why you wouldn't want to store them." She was looking at the bed.

"Pieces of what? Pieces of cheese?" Mrs. Kevin-Spending stood up, plucking delicately at the seat of her velvet pants. "Take your big foot off that book," she said to me. I did so. "Study your Irregular Futures." She started for the kitchenette. "I had a magnificent credenza at one time, if that's what you mean," she said. "Crotch mahogany, whatever that is." I picked up my French book and opened it. Teddy was trying to catch my eye and I, with my neck getting hot, was trying to prevent her. Mrs. Kevin-Spending was back.

"What's that?" she demanded. She was pointing with a stiff-fingered, outflung arm. The beads she'd had in her hand were skipping over the floor and Teddy and I were out of our chairs, scared. She wanted us to look at the lamp. We looked at it—hard. Made out of a samovar, it had an ugly shade, brown panels with scenes cut out on them. After a while we looked at her.

"The Left Bank!" she said triumphantly. "Do you see that?" Her gesture was tremendous. It introduced a blurry shawl flung over her piano.

"Pretty," Teddy said. "Our grandmother has one." She started to sit down, but Mrs. Kevin-Spending caught her right arm and detained her. With the other hand she took my wrist.

"Do you hear her?" she said to me. "Her grandmother! Doesn't she know where I got those? Paris! Her grandmother, no less."

"Well, actually, she's both of our grandmothers," Teddy said huffily.

She took a step backward, but Mrs. Kevin-Spending wouldn't let go. "There was the darlingest side street, the darlingest shop," she said, "and I saw those and Valentine said, 'You *want* it? *Buy* it!' That's just the way he was— 'You *want* it? *Buy* it!' I got those in Paris, too." She steered us around to face a fretwork shelf. On it were a peeling gilt replica of the Eiffel Tower and a manikin pis. " 'You *want* it? *Buy* it!' " she said, laughing. " '*Buy* it!' " She let go of us and swung her arms, raising freedom and largess.

Teddy sat down. "I'm going to Paris," she said, shaking back a wing of her long blond hair. "My grandmother's taking me."

Mrs. Kevin-Spending smiled. "All young girls think they'll get to Paris."

"I'm going. No gaff." Teddy gave her a steady look.

"Is Isolde going, too?"

"It's a different grandmother," I said aloofly. "I'm not

_____

207

going anyplace." I sat down again on my hard straight chair. The only place I wanted to go was home, wherever that was. But Mrs. Kevin-Spending gave me a friendly squeeze.

"Neither am I," she said. "But there's no reason why a schoolgirl and an elderly lady mightn't have a pleasant, educative little tour, I suppose." She put her hand on the back of my neck, under my heavy hair. I felt myself drawn into a conspiracy of superior perception.

"Bubbles isn't old," Teddy said. "She rockets around like nobody's business."

"Bubbles is old," I said, with Mrs. Kevin-Spending's arm around me. "Don't kid yourself. Bubbles is plenty old."

Mrs. Kevin-Spending patted me and went over to sit on the bed. "We bought such a lot," she said dreamily. "We had a house, the most marvelous house, so adorably furnished. And several Wallace Nuttings that were heirlooms. And a vast green lawn with a Winston crab apple tree." She smiled at me. "Have you ever seen a Winston crab apple tree? You'd adore it."

Teddy crossed her legs. "Are we going to speak French, or what?"

"In due course or a little later," Mrs. Kevin-Spending said. "Don't anybody start till I'm ready."

"Was that in France, or where, that apple tree?" I said.

"In Horseheads," Mrs Kevin-Spending said, with a heavy-lidded look of rapture. "Near Elmira."

"Horse *what?*" Teddy said.

"Horseheads. A very historical site. General Sullivan led his historic march from wherever it was to Dover, New Jersey, and on the way they camped at Horseheads. Well, in the middle of the night the Indians crept up and lopped off all the horses' heads. And that's how Horseheads got its name."

"What do people do in a place like that?" Teddy said. "It sounds sort of bare of advantages to me."

Mrs. Kevin-Spending pulled off one of her earrings and held it so it sparkled in the scalding light. "They clean the sto-ove," she said crooningly. "They wake up in the morning and they say, 'This is the day the Lord hath made.'" She tossed the earring in the air and clapped her hands and caught it, like a girl playing jacks. "They read books like *An Englishwoman's Love Letters*," she added in an elevated tone. "You've never read that, I suppose."

"Well, who wrote it?" Teddy said gamely.

"An Englishwoman, I should imagine. Valentine was a writer himself. He wrote the most marvelous play about old Spain. Every time I think of that pavilion scene, I cry." She found her earring and screwed it on again. "Valentine was a wonderful raconteur," she said. "He had people laughing all the time. He had a little blue book with just the last lines of amusing anecdotes written down in it. The *punch* lines. 'Women are angels without any wings,' he used to say, 'and yet they are very pec-u-liar things'—oh, he was witty."

"Somebody told me your husband taught hygiene in Poughkeepsie," Teddy said, pulling up her socks. She gave me a fractional glance to see how I was taking that. I wasn't taking it well. Neither was Mrs. Kevin-Spending.

"My second husband," she said, after a minute. "He comes here weekends, some weekends. He sleeps in the vestibule. Come on," she said. "I'll show you."

She led us to the hall. Beneath a lavabo stuffed with rhododendron, bronzing, dusty, and tightly furled in

---

209

death, stood a folding cot, its handles left exposed by an old purple blanket. None of us got very close to it. Mrs. Kevin-Spending pressed the mattress with the tips of her fingers. The springs gave a sigh, as of sorrows bravely borne. People were shrieking at each other in the next apartment.

"It looks very comfortable," Teddy said.

"Sterling," Mrs. Kevin-Spending said, wiping her hand on her pants.

We filed back into the other room. "Don't wiggle your hips, Teresa, it doesn't in the least become you," Mrs. Kevin-Spending said. "I'm going to make some cocoa now. The bathroom's that door there."

The bathroom was a searing pink, the fixtures politely upholstered in chenille. Teddy checked her profile in the mirror and gave herself a couple of sharp slaps under the chin with the back of her hand. Then she looked in my direction. I was sitting on the edge of the tub, somberly regarding the bath mat, a rectangle embroidered with the outlines of one very large and one very small bare foot.

"I suppose you like that? Well, I think it's *fey,*" Teddy said. Waiting for the impact of her opinion to subside, she opened the medicine cabinet. Inside was an expensive chaos. Teddy found a chin strap and tied it on. She anointed herself with a pale green paste.

"You know Mimi Schrott's sister?" Her diction was poor on account of the chin strap.

"No!" I said. A long-handled bath brush, worn and woefully intimate, lay along the back rim of the tub. A bright blue douche bag was suspended from the shower ring. A ballerina in a glued-on tutu straddled a jar full of purple pellets that might have been for anything but certainly looked like worm cure.

"Mimi Schrott's sister goes to this very rotch school where her husband teaches."

"Whose husband?" I said ferociously. "*Whose* husband?"

"The Princess of Pure Delight's. And his name is Mr. Ziff."

"If I didn't know that, I couldn't live through the night."

"*Ziff*. He has a tic." Teddy demonstrated, with an involved and graphic jiggle, the probable severity of Mr. Ziff's affliction. "Horseheads," she said, "I never heard of anything so stinking middle-class." She puffed out her cheeks and tapped lightly along her jaw. Upward so as not to wreck her contours. "I like her crazy shoes, though. Those red heels are whorey."

"(A)," I said severely, "they are not. (B), the *w* is silent." I got up, regally, and left, banging my hipbone on the jamb of the door.

· · ·

Mrs. Kevin-Spending had set a table with squarish, painted china. When Teddy came out of the bathroom, she brought cocoa and a plate of wet tan cake. Teddy reached for a piece and Mrs. Kevin-Spending stamped her foot. "Serve Isolde first," she said. "Don't be such an opportunist." It was miserable cake. Teddy plied me with it all evening.

"These are pretty dishes," Teddy said peaceably, watching me chew.

"Yes?" Mrs. Kevin-Spending said. "Well, just remember

that they're Swiss and they mustn't get broken." She snatched a pillow from behind Teddy and settled on it on the floor, in a pose that made conversation and even swallowing very difficult.

"If my mother could see you sitting on the floor, she'd take off like a big black bird," Teddy said.

"Your mother is a big bird," I said. "If you want to know."

"I'm ready to start speaking French," Teddy said.

"My mother's worse," I said. "She gets you in Wanamakers and asks you questions about your sex life. She's got a Noguchi table, which is the crux, for all she knows."

"I wish we could start speaking French," Teddy said.

"*Servez-vous de gâteau,*" Mrs. Kevin-Spending said frugally. "It's gingerbread and it's delicious." She drew her knees up and put her arms around them. "I used to make marvelous cabbage rolls," she said sadly, "but Sterling says they're gassy. Drink your chocolate and I'll tell you my dreams. The other night I dreamed a poem—'squatty little nightsheds, bearing down on sleep.' There was more, but that's all I remember. Like 'I have a little shadow that goes in and out with me'—only worse." She extended her arms in front of her, bent her elbows parallel to the floor, grasped in each hand the opposite forearm, and pushed. An execution familiar to both Teddy and myself, it was designed to modify, enlarge, or merely maintain the bosom. "I can just see them," she said, not stopping, "a hillside full of nightsheds, advancing like an army, with little pointed roofs."

"Mimi Schrott's sister goes to Ferncliffe and she knows Mr. Ziff," Teddy said.

Mrs. Kevin-Spending dropped her arms. She looked as

though it were a long time since a piece of information of quite so little interest had come her way. "I could play the piano for you if I wanted," she said. "But I don't. Don't coax." She got up and went to the piano. She spun the stool and sat down with her back to the keyboard. "Middle C is jammed, anyway," she said. "Anybody here play euchre? I thought not. I used to play euchre every night of my life. The knave of trumps is right bower. Valentine inevitably won." She ran her fingers through her fluffy silver hair. "Sterling plays the oboe. He leaves these objects sitting around in glasses of water that look like I don't know what."

"Oh, reeds," Teddy said. "They're for the mouthpiece."

"I know what they are and I know what they're for and it doesn't console me. He also plays the cello and the classical guitar. He's learning Russian from phonograph records and he's an amateur palmist." A sprinkling of the beads she'd dropped lay on the floor around her. She stepped on them, one by one, efficiently and almost with alarm. "Sterling has many admirable qualities," she said. She paused and reflected, seeming to be about to run through them, but apparently they eluded her. "He has a sort of a declivity in his forehead. Not a *hole*. Nothing a stranger would even notice. But there it is. And his jaw clicks. When he chews. Just on one side—the left side. Not *loudly*, but all the time. I mean, you're sitting there and you know it's going to happen and it does. His mother carried him for nine and three-quarter months and then he was born feet first." She spun around and poked at a little brass castle on the piano's top. "I'd burn some incense," she said. "If I *had* some incense." She spun around again. It was evidently a maneuver she enjoyed. "I have a big blue ugly on my leg," she said newsily. "See it?"

213

She hiked up the leg of her pants and showed us the mauvish squiggle of a broken vein. "It's none of those things," she said, hiding it again. "Valentine used to wear these apricot-colored crepe-soled shoes. They were terrible shoes. My father used to call them brothel creepers. But I never minded them. He had this Afghan dog named Cassius that smelled like low tide and threw up under the stove just to spite me. And I never minded that. Because with Valentine everything was terribly requited." She leaned toward us, poised on her piano stool, immediate and full of secrets. "He bought me this giddy hat once. It had half a bird on it and it was gorgeous, but it was awful. I looked horrible in it and I wore it all the time." She was laughing. "And once he brought home 'The Last Supper' made out of butterfly wings. If Sterling did that, I'd call the police. But," she said realistically, "Sterling wouldn't do it." She took a metronome off the piano, wound it, and set it ticking on her knee. "Valentine was nice," she said, in a different way. "He used to put marigolds in our tea. He used to get terrible cold sores." She looked at us with wide tearbright eyes. "Oh, Heaven's Judgment, that's what I'd like to teach," she said. "Not French."

"Excuse me?" Teddy said.

Mrs. Kevin-Spending seemed hard-pressed. She stopped the metronome without looking at it. "There's danger. There's risk. Either the world hatches out like a big egg, or it doesn't. And if it doesn't, well, don't come crying to me."

"How could a person be careful, though?" I asked her. "I mean, exactly how?" I had the feeling that something important was happening to me, but as was usual in my life, I didn't know what.

Mrs. Kevin-Spending didn't say a word. All of a sudden

I remembered something. It was just a thing about my father, that happened when I was young, but it broke in my head like a private, interior skyrocket.

"One time my father mowed the lawn in the rain," I told her. "In the middle of the night, I mean. In the rain."

"He did?" she said. She smiled with what I took to be high-level comprehension.

"My mother kept telling him to mow the lawn," I said quickly. "And he kept getting furious. And he went slamming out. He didn't come home for dinner or anything. When I woke up in the middle of the night, there was thunder and lightning and you could hear the lawn mower going like mad. My mother was kneeling at the top of the stairs. I could see her right from my bed. She was wearing this yellow nightgown she had and she was watching my father and laughing like mad. Not out loud. She never even knew I saw her."

Mrs. Kevin-Spending darted from her stool and spooned sugar into the dregs of my cocoa. I kept remembering my parents that night, fooling around in the kitchen when they thought I was asleep, playing "Whispering" on an old wind-up phonograph. Maybe they were dancing, I wouldn't know. "Whispering," a terrible song, sounded good that night.

Mrs. Kevin-Spending showed up carrying two dolls. "Look at these," she said, dumping them in my lap. "You'll adore them. They're for Sterling's British cousin's child. I adore children and it's a pity they make me so nervous. But they're so opinionated." She began to bounce an imaginary ball, pointing her toe for the leg-overs. " 'On the mountain stands a lady/ who she is I do not know/ all she wants is gold and silver' . . . something, something, something-so."

" 'All she wants is a rich young beau,' " Teddy said, filling in the somethings.

"I'm terribly sorry, but you're wrong! You remind me terribly of Sterling's British cousin's child. Gold and silver, Isolde," she said, giving me a jab in the ribs. "Sit up straight, don't hunch over like that." She seized a double handful of my hair. "All of this cut off, a nice thick Empire bang." She put her hands in her pockets and stood back, searching out, with something less than happy expectation, further measures. "Could you see your way clear to having about a foot taken off your winter coat?"

"I've thought about it," I said, "I really have. But everybody dresses like that in Philadelphia."

"Do you come from Philadelphia?" Mrs. Kevin-Spending said jubilantly. "How nice! Wear your darling tweed coat to class tomorrow and I'll fix it for you. I made this costume I'm wearing out of some portieres." She made a preening pirouette. "Don't you love the color? Absinthe!" She looked seriously at me again. "You know what else, Iseult? I think if you could inject a little more abandon into your personality, that would help."

"It sure would," Teddy said.

I was in the spirit of the thing by that time. "Okay," I said.

"Try," she said. "Remember gold and silver. Try."

"Is gold and silver money?" Teddy said.

"Because it can happen to quite ordinary people," Mrs. Kevin-Spending said mystically. "People with big noses, people who spit when they talk. I've seen it. I look for it, all the time."

"Does gold and silver mean money?" Teddy said.

———

"It means splendor!" Mrs. Kevin-Spending said. She smote herself dramatically on the chest, but she didn't look foolish to me. "He's dead," she said. "You can't do a thing about that. If there was anything you could do about that, you'd make a fortune. But *you're* not dead."

I had a small experience of splendor at that time. The most splendid thing I could think of was my mother in her yellow nightgown, but it seemed to do. I felt wise and brave and, for a change, onto the order of things. Mrs. Kevin-Spending spoiled it.

"He hung himself," she said.

"Oh, my goodness," Teddy said.

Mrs. Kevin-Spending sat down on the bed. She tucked one foot beneath her and rested her cheek against a post. It was a girlish attitude, but she looked old. "And so did Cassius," she said. "Two months before, on the second of June. I took him for his walk and I put him in the car afterward, for his nap. I always did that. But I left his collar and his leash on him and he got tangled up some way. He hung himself on the handle of the door. And Valentine found him." Her eyes moved around the room. "I detested that dog. Valentine doted on Cassius, but he never said a word in reproach."

I saw reflected, in her long-lashed, aging eyes, my mother, dusting her Noguchi table, and my fat aunt wound around with sweet potato vines—and most of the women who went to Paris and most of the others who didn't. Tear-distorted, dippy, beleaguered, bereft, there they were: beautiful, silly, unlucky, plain, much too smart or far from smart enough.

The room was still, but not for long. Mrs. Kevin-Spending hopped off the bed and came over to take the dolls from my lap. "Well," she said cheerily, "this one's from France and this one's from Spain. I've never been to Spain." She held out the dolls and there was a terrible minute when she might have been going to give them to me.

"I have a huge collection of stuffed animals," Teddy said. "I have a panda as big as a three-year-old child that Ruthie Lambert's brother gave me."

Mrs. Kevin-Spending plumped out the skirts of the dolls and shifted them both to one arm. "Ruthie Lambert has body odor of the breath," she said. "Does her brother have it, too?"

She glanced at her watch. We rose as though a bell had rung and were shooed out into the hall. She walked with us to the top of the steps. "Good night," she said, "good night, ladies."

Teddy started down. I followed her for two steps and then I stopped and craned around. "I think you have a very beautiful apartment," I said. "I think you've had a very, very fascinating life."

She stood at the top of the stairs and kissed her fingers at us until we turned on the landing. "Be careful of trolls on the stairs," she called, "be careful."

I was very careful. I could hear her red heels clattering, back to her open door and beyond it, the world—wide, bright, and as perilous as I'd suspected.

•   •   •

The night was black outside. The block lay long ahead of us, thick with maple trees and jeopardy. We passed a Colonial-style funeral parlor. Ghastly blue spotlights played on its pillared facade. Teddy caught hold of my belt. "I don't know if I told you," she said, "I'm flushing that panda. And I'm checking Dougie Lambert out. He says, 'Take a shave.' I can't stand anybody that says that." We began to giggle. Teddy jumped up, using me for leverage, and snapped a pol- lydoodle off a maple tree. She broke it and fixed the gluey end on the bridge of her nose. Then she stuck the other half on my nose, walking backward to do it. They rode there, two frail green single wings, two totems.

———

About the Author

Ellen Currie is the author of one previous book, *Available Light*. Her short fiction has been published in *The New Yorker* and other magazines. She lives in Pennington, New Jersey.